## UTOPIA: 1973

The world would be a far different place if it weren't torn and bloodied by constant wars. There would be so much less human suffering, and who knows what wonders might be accomplished if all mankind remained at peace?

In this exciting and inventive novel, Michael Moorcock tells of a man who visited such a world. The year is 1973, and there have been no wars at all since 1910. Technology, commerce, international politics have developed without interference from warfare.

It's a new Utopia—or is it? For there is a shadow over even this bright tomorrow, and it is growing. Is a disastrous war truly inevitable?

MICHAEL MOORCOCK has shown his versatility as the author of many popular science fiction and fantasy novels ranging from outright fantasy adventure (the "Elric" series) through witty speculative farces (THE FINAL PROGRAMME) to romantic stories of the far future (THE ICE SCHOONER). He won the Nebula Award in 1968 for his short novel *Behold the Man*, and for the past eight years has been editor of the unorthodox British sf magazine *New Worlds*.

He lives in London with his wife, writer Hilary Bailey, and their three children.

# THE
# WARLORD
# OF THE AIR

## A Scientific Romance

## by Michael Moorcock

ACE BOOKS

A Division of Charter Communications Inc.
1120 Avenue of the Americas
New York, N. Y. 10036

DEDICATION:

*For Julie.*

*Interior illustrations by
James Cawthorn.*

"The War is ceaseless. The most we can hope for are occasional moments of tranquility in the midst of the conflict."

— *Lobkowitz*

## EDITOR'S NOTE

I never met my grandfather Michael Moorcock and knew very little of him until my grandmother's death last year when I was given a box of his papers by my father. "These seem to be more in your line than mine," he said. "I didn't know we had another scribbler in the family." Most of the papers were diaries, the beginnings of essays and short stories, some conventional Edwardian poetry—and a typewritten manuscript which, without further comment, we publish here, perhaps a little later than he would have hoped.

Michael Moorcock
Ladbroke Grove
London.
January 1971.

## CONTENTS

# BOOK ONE

## HOW AN ENGLISH ARMY OFFICER ENTERED THE WORLD OF THE FUTURE AND WHAT HE SAW THERE

### CHAPTER I

### The Opium Eater of Rowe Island

IN THE SPRING of 1903, on the advice of my physician, I had occasion to visit that remote and beautiful fragment of land in the middle of the Indian Ocean which I shall call Rowe Island. I had been overworking and had contracted what the quacks now like to term 'exhaustion' or even 'nervous debility'. In other words I was completely whacked out and needed a rest a long way away from anywhere. I had a small interest in the mining company which is the sole industry of the island (unless you count Religion!) and I knew that its climate was ideal, as was its location—one of the healthiest places in the world and fifteen hundred miles from any form of civilisation. So I purchased my ticket, packed my boxes, bade farewell to my nearest and dearest, and boarded the liner which would take me to Jakarta. From Jakarta, after a pleasant and uneventful voyage, I took one of the company boats to Rowe Island. I had managed the journey in less than a month.

Rowe Island has no business to be where it is. There is nothing near it. There is nothing to indicate that it is there. You come upon it suddenly, rising out of the water like the tip of some vast underwater mountain (which, in fact, it is). It is a great wedge of volcanic rock surrounded by a shimmering sea which resembles burnished metal when it is still or boiling silver and molten steel when it is testy. The rock is about twelve miles long by five miles across and is thickly wooded in places, bare and severe in other parts. Everything goes uphill until it reaches the top and then, on the other side of the hill, the rock simply falls away, down and down into the sea a thousand feet below.

Built around the harbour is a largish town which, as you approach it, resembles nothing so much as a prosperous Devon fishing village—until you see the Malay and Chinese buildings behind the facades of the hotels and offices which line the quayside. There is room in the harbour for several good sized steamers and a number of sailing vessels, principally native dhows and junks which are used for fishing. Further up the hill you can see the workings of the mines which employ the greatest part of the population which is Malay and Chinese labourers and their wives and families. Prominent on the quayside are the warehouses and offices of the Welland Rock Phosphate Mining Company and the great white and gold facade of the Royal Habour Hotel of which the proprietor is one Minheer Olmeijer, a Dutchman from Surabaya. There are also an almost ungodly number of missions, Buddhist temples, Malay mosques and shrines of more mysterious origin. There are several less ornate hotels than Olmeijer's, there are general stores, sheds and buildings which serve the tiny railway which brings the ore down from the mountain and along the quayside. There are three hospitals, two of which are for natives only. I say 'natives' in the loose sense. There were no natives of any sort before the island was settled thirty years ago by the people who founded the Welland firm; all labour was brought from the Peninsula, mainly from Singapore. On a hill to the south of the harbour, standing rather aloof from the town and dominating it, is the residence of the Official Representative, Brigadier Bland, together with the barracks which houses the small garrison of native police under the command of a very upright servant of the Empire, Lieutenant Allsop. Over this spick and span collection of whitewashed stucco flies a proud Union Jack, symbol of protection and justice to all who dwell on the island.

Unless you are fond of paying an endless succession of social calls on the other English people, most of whom can talk only of mining or of missions, there is not a great deal to do on Rowe Island. There is an amateur dramatic society which puts on a play at the Official Representative's residence every Christmas, there is a club of sorts where one may play billiards if invited by the oldest members (I was invited once but played rather badly). The local newspapers from Singapore, Sarawak or Sydney are almost always at least a fortnight old, when you can find them, the *Times* is a month to six weeks old and the illustrated weeklies and monthly journals from home can be anything up to six months old by the time you see them. This sparsity of up-to-date news is, of course, a very good thing for a man recovering from exhaustion. It is hard to get hot under the collar about a war which has been over a month or two before you read about it or a stock market tremor which has resolved itself one way or the other by the previous week. You are forced to relax. After all, there is nothing you can do to alter the course of what has become history. But it is when you have begun to recover your energy, both mental and physical, that you begin to realise how bored you are—and within two months this realisation had struck me most forcibly. I began to nurse a rather evil hope that something would happen on Rowe Island—an explosion in the mine, an earthquake, or perhaps even a native uprising.

In this frame of mind I took to haunting the harbour, watching the ships loading and unloading, with long lines of coolies carrying sacks of corn and rice away from the quayside or guiding the trucks of phosphate up the

11

gangplanks to dump them in the empty holds. I was surprised to see so many women doing work which in England few would have thought women *could* do! Some of these women were quite young and some were almost beautiful. The noise was almost deafening when a ship or several ships were in port. Naked brown and yellow bodies milled everywhere, like so much churning mud, sweating in the intense heat—a heat relieved only by the breezes off the sea.

It was on one such day that I found myself down by the harbour, having had my lunch at Olmeijer's hotel, where I was staying, watching a steamer ease her way towards the quay, blowing her whistle at the junks and dhows which teemed around her. Like so many of the ships which ply that part of the world, she was sturdy but unlovely to look upon. Her hull and superstructure were battered and needed painting and her crew, mainly laskars, seemed as if they would have been more at home on some Malay pirate ship. I saw the captain, an elderly Scot, cursing at them from his bridge and bellowing incoherently through a megaphone while a half-caste mate seemed to be performing some peculiar, private dance of his own amongst the seamen. The ship was the *Maria Carlson* bringing provisions and, I hoped, some mail. She berthed at last and I began to push my way through the coolies towards her, hoping she had brought me some letters and the journals which I had begged my brother to send me from London.

The mooring ropes were secured, the anchor dropped and the gangplanks lowered and then the half-caste mate, his cap on the back of his head, his jacket open, came springing down, howling at the coolies who gathered there waving the scraps of paper they had received at the hiring office. As he howled he gathered up the papers and waved wildly at the ship, presumably issuing instructions. I hailed him with my cane.

"Any mail?" I called.

"Mail? Mail?" He offered me a look of hatred and contempt which I took for a negative reply to my question. Then he rushed back up the gangplank and disappeared. I waited, however, in the hope of seeing the captain and confirming with him that there was, indeed, no mail. Then I saw a white man appear at the top of the gangplank, pausing and staring blankly around him as if he had not expected to find land on the other side of the rail at all. Someone gave him a shove from behind and he staggered down the bouncing plank, fell at the bottom and picked himself up in time to catch the small seabag which the mate threw to him from the ship.

The man was dressed in a filthy linen suit, had no hat, no shirt. He was unshaven and there were native sandles on his feet. I had seen his type before. Some wretch whom the East had ruined, who had discovered a weakness within himself which he might never have found if he had stayed safely at home in England. As he straightened up, however, I was startled by an expression of intense misery in his eyes, a certain dignity of bearing which was not at all common in the type. He shouldered his bag and began to make his way towards the town.

"And don't try to get back aboard, mister, or the law will have you next time!" screamed the mate of the *Maria Carlson* after him. The down-and-out hardly seemed to hear. He continued to plod along the quayside, jostled by the coolies, frantic for work.

The mate saw me and gesticulated impatiently. "No mail. No mail."

I decided to believe him, but called: "Who is that chap? What's he done?"

"Stowaway," was the curt reply.

I wondered why anyone should want to stow away on a ship bound for Rowe Island and on impulse I turned and followed the man. For some reason I believed him to be no ordinary derelict and he had piqued my curiosity. Besides, my boredom was so great that I should have welcomed any relief from it. Also I was sure that there *was* something different about his eyes and his bearing and that, if I could encourage him to confide in me, he would have an interesting story to tell. Perhaps I felt sorry for him, too. Whatever the reason, I hastened to catch him up and address him.

"Don't be offended," I said, "but you look to me as if you could make some use of a square meal and maybe a drink."

"Drink?"

He turned those strange, tormented eyes on me as if he had recognised me as the Devil himself. "Drink?"

"You look all up, old chap." I could hardly bear to look into that face, so great was the agony I saw there. "You'd better come with me."

Unresistingly, he let me lead him down the harbour road until we reached Olmeijer's. The Indian servants in the lobby weren't happy about my bringing in such an obvious derelict, but I led him straight upstairs to my suite and ordered my houseboy to start a bath at once. In the meantime I sat my guest down in my best chair and asked him what he would like to drink.

He shrugged. "Anything. Rum?"

I poured him a stiffish shot of rum and handed him the glass. He downed it in a couple of swallows and nodded his thanks. He sat placidly in the chair, his hands folded in his lap, staring at the table.

His accent, though distant and bemused, had been that of a cultivated man—a gentleman—and this aroused my curiosity even further.

"Where are you from?" I asked him. "Singapore?"

"From?" He gave me an odd look and then frowned to himself. He muttered something which I could not catch and then the houseboy entered and told me that he had prepared the bath.

"The bath's ready," I said. "If you'd like to use it I'll be looking out one of my suits. We're about the same size."

He rose like an automaton and followed the houseboy into the bathroom, but then he re-emerged almost at once. "My bag," he said.

I picked up the bag from the floor and handed it to him. He went back into the bathroom and closed the door.

The houseboy looked curiously at me. "Is he some—some relative, sahib?"

I laughed. "No, Ram Dass. He is just a man I found on the quay."

Ram Dass smiled. "Aha! It is the Christian charity." He seemed satisfied. As a recent convert (the pride of one of the local missions) he was constantly translating all the mysterious actions of the English into good, simple Christian terms. "He is a beggar, then? You are the Samaritan?"

"I'm not sure I'm as selfless as that," I told him. "Will you fetch one of my suits for the gentleman to put on after he has had his bath?"

Ram Dass nodded enthusiastically. "And a shirt, and a tie, and socks, and shoes—everything?"

I was amused. "Very well. Everything."

My guest took a very long time about his ablutions, but came out of the bathroom at last looking much more spruce than when he had gone in. Ram Dass had dressed him in my clothes and they fitted extraordinarily well, though a little loose, for I was considerably better fed than he. Ram Dass behind him brandished a razor as bright as his grin. "I have shaved the gentleman, sahib!"

The man before me was a good-looking young man in his late twenties, although there was something about the set of his features which occasionally made him look much older. He had golden wavy hair, a good jaw and a firm mouth. He had none of the usual signs of weakness which I had learned to recognise in the others of his kind I had seen. Some of the pain had gone out of his eyes, but had been replaced by an even more remote—even dreamy—expression. It was Ram Dass, sniffing significantly and holding up a long, carved pipe behind the man, who gave me the clue.

So that was it! My guest was an opium eater! He was

addicted to a drug which some had called the Curse of the Orient, which contributed much to that familiar attitude of fatalism we equate with the East, which robbed men of their will to eat, to work, to indulge in any of the usual pleasures with which others beguile their hours—a drug which eventually kills them.

With an effort I managed to control any expression of horror or pity which I might feel and said instead:

"Well, old chap, what do you say to a late lunch?"

"If you wish it," he said distantly.

"I should have thought you were hungry."

"Hungry? No."

"Well, at any rate, we'll get something brought up. Ram Dass? Could you arrange for some food? Perhaps something cold. And tell Mnr. Olmeijer that I shall have a guest staying the night. We'll need sheets for the other bed and so on."

Ram Dass went away and, uninvited, my guest crossed to the sideboard and helped himself to a large whisky. He hesitated for a moment before pouring in some soda. It was almost as if he were trying to remember how to prepare a drink.

"Where were you making for when you stowed away?" I asked. "Surely not Rowe Island?"

He turned, sipping his drink and staring through the window at the sea beyond the harbour. "This is Rowe Island?"

"Yes. The end of the world in many respects."

"The what?" He looked at me suspiciously and I saw a hint of that torment in his eyes again.

"I was speaking figuratively. Not much to do on Rowe Island. Nowhere to go, really, except back where you came from. Where did you come from, by the way?"

He gestured vaguely. "I see. Yes. Oh, Japan, I suppose."

"Japan? You were in the foreign service there, perhaps?"

He looked at me intently as if he thought my words

16

had some hidden meaning. Then he said: "Before that, India. Yes, India before that. I was in the Army."

"How—?" I was embarrassed. "How did you come to be aboard the *Maria Carlson*—the ship which brought you here?"

He shrugged. "I'm afraid I don't remember. Since I left—since I came back—it has been like a dream. Only the damned opium helps me forget. Those dreams are less horrifying."

"You take opium?" I felt like a hypocrite, framing the question like that.

"As much as I can get hold of."

"You seem to have been through some rather terrible experience," I said, forgetting my manners completely.

He laughed then, more in self-mockery than at me. "Yes! Yes. It turned me mad. That's what you'd think, anyway. What's the date, by the way?"

He was becoming more communicative as he downed his third drink.

"It's the 29th of May," I told him.

"What year?"

"Why, 1903!"

"I knew that really. I knew it." He spoke defensively now. "1903, of course. The beginning of a bright new century—perhaps even the last century of the world."

From another man, I might have taken these disconnected ramblings to be merely the crazed utterances of the opium fiend, but from him they seemed oddly convincing. I decided it was time to introduce myself and did so.

He chose a peculiar way in which to respond to this introduction. He drew himself up and said: "This is Captain Oswald Bastable, late of the 53rd Lancers." He smiled at this private joke and went and sat down in an armchair near the window.

A moment later, while I was still trying to recover myself, he turned his head and looked up at me in amusement. "I'm sorry, but you see I'm in a mood not

17

to try to disguise my madness. You're very kind." He raised his glass in a salute. "I thank you. I must try to remember my manners. I had some once. They were a fine set of manners. Couldn't be beaten, I dare say. But I could introduce myself in several ways. What if I said my name was Oswald Bastable—Airshipman."

"You fly balloons?"

"I have flown *airships*, sir. Ships twelve-hundred feet long which travel at speeds *in excess of one hundred miles an hour!* You see. I am mad."

"Well, I would say you were inventive, if nothing else. Where did you fly the airships?"

"Oh, most parts of the world."

"I must be completely out of touch. I knew I was receiving the news rather late, but I'm afraid I haven't heard of these ships. When did you make the flight?"

Bastable's opium-filled eyes stared at me so hard that I shuddered.

"Would you really care to hear?" he said in a cold, small voice.

My mouth felt dry and I wondered if he were about to become violent. I moved toward the bell-rope. But he knew what was in my mind because he laughed again and shook his head. "I won't attack you, sir. But you see now why I smoke opium, why I know myself to be mad. Who but a madman would claim to have flown through the skies faster than the fastest ocean liner? Who but a madman would claim to have done this in the year 1973 A.D?—nearly three quarters of a century in the future?"

"You believe that you have done this? And no one will listen to you. Is that what makes you so bitter?"

"That? No! Why should it? It is the thought of my own folly which torments me. I should be dead—that would be just. But instead I am half-alive, hardly knowing one dream from another, one reality from another."

I took his empty glass from his hand and filled it for him. "Look here," I said. "If you will do something for me, I'll agree to listen to what you have to say. There's precious little else for me to do, anyway."

"What do you want me to do?"

"I want you to eat some lunch and try to stay off the opium for a while—until you've seen a doctor, at least. Then I want you to agree that you'll put yourself in my care, perhaps even return with me to England when I go back. Will you do that?"

"Perhaps." He shrugged. "But this mood could pass, I warn you. I've never had the inclination to speak to anyone about—about the airships and everything. Yet, perhaps history is alterable. . . ."

"I don't follow you."

"If I told you what I know, what happened to me—what I saw—it might make a difference. If you agreed to write it down, publish it, if you could, when you got back."

"When *we* got back," I said firmly.

"Just as you like." His expression altered, became grim, as if his decision had a significance I had not understood.

And so the lunch was brought up and he ate some of the cold chicken and the salad. The meal seemed to do him good, for he became more coherent.

"I'll try to begin at the beginning," he said, "and go through to the end—telling it as it happened."

I had a large notebook and several pencils by me. In the early days of my career I had earned my living as a Parliamentary Reporter and my knowledge of short-hand stood me in good stead as Bastable began to speak.

He told me his story over the next three days, in which time we scarcely left that room, scarcely slept. Occasionally Bastable would revive himself by recourse to some pills he had—which he swore to me were not opium—but I needed no other stimulant than Bastable's story itself. The atmosphere in that hotel room became unreal as the tale unfolded. I began by thinking I listened to the fantastic ravings of a madman but I ended by believing without any doubt that I had heard the truth—or, at least, *a* truth. It is up to you to decide if what follows is fiction or not. I can only assure you that Bastable said it was not fiction and I believe, profoundly, that he was right.

Michael Moorcock
Three Chimneys
Mitcham, Surrey.
October 1904.

# CHAPTER II

## The Temple at Teku Benga

I DON'T KNOW if you've ever been in North East India (began Bastable) but if you have you'll know what I mean when I say it's the meeting place of worlds both old and immeasurably ancient. Where India, Nepaul, Tibet and Bhutan come together, about two hundred miles north of Darjiling and about a hundred west of Mt. Kinchunmaja, you'll find Kumbalari: a state which claims to be older than Time. It's what they call a 'Theocracy'—priest-ridden in the extreme, full of dark superstitions and darker myths and legends, where all gods and demons are honoured, doubtless to be on the safe side. The people are cruel, ignorant, dirty and proud—they look down their noses at all other races. They resent the British presence so close to their territory and over the past couple of hundred years we've had a spot or two of trouble with them, but never anything much. They won't go far beyond their own borders, luckily, and their population is kept pretty low thanks to their own various barbaric practises. Sometimes, as on this occasion, a religious leader pops up who convinces them of the necessity of some kind of jehad against the British or British protected peoples, tells them they're impervious to our bullets and so forth, and we have to go and teach them a lesson. They are not regarded very seriously by the Army, which is doubtless why I was put in charge of the expedition which, in 1902, set off for the Himalayas and Kumbalari.

It was the first time I had commanded so many men and I felt my responsibility very seriously. I had a squadron of a hundred and fifty sowars of the impressive Punjabi Lancers and two hundred fierce, loyal little sepoys of the 9th Ghoorka Infantry. I was intensely proud of my army and felt that if it had had to it could have conquered the whole of Bengal. I was, of course, the only white officer, but I was perfectly willing to admit that the native officers were men of much greater experience than myself and whenever possible I relied on their advice.

My orders were to make a show of strength and, if I could, to avoid a scrap. We just wanted to give the beggars an idea of what they would come up against if we started to take them seriously. Their latest leader —an old fanatic by the name of Sharan Kang—was their King, Archbishop and C-in-C all rolled into one. Sharan Kang had already burned one of our frontier stations and killed a couple of detachments of Native Police. We weren't interested in vengeance, however, but in making sure it didn't go any further.

We had some reasonably good maps and a couple of fairly trustworthy guides—distant kinsmen of the Ghoorkas—and we reckoned it would take us little more than two or three days to get to Teku Benga, which was Sharan Kang's capital, high up in the mountains and reached by a series of narrow passes. Since we were on a diplomatic rather than a military mission, we showed great care in displaying a flag of truce as we crossed the borders into Kumbalari, whose bleak, snow-streaked mountains lowered down at us on all sides.

It was not long before we had our first glimpse of

some Kumbalaris. They sat on shaggy ponies which were perched like goats on high mountain ledges: squat, yellow-skinned warriors all swathed in leather and sheepskin and painted iron, their slitted eyes gleaming with hatred and suspicion. If these were not the descendants of Attila the Hun, then they were the descendants of some even earlier warrior folk which had fought on these slopes and gorges a thousand or two thousand years before the Scourge of God had led his hordes East and West, to pillage three quarters of the known world. Like their ancestors, these were armed with bows, lances, scimitars, but they also had a few carbines, probably of Russian origin.

Pretending to ignore these watching riders, I led my soldiers up the valley. I had a moment's surprise when a few shots rang out from above and echoed on and on through the peaks, but the guides assured me that these were merely signals to announce our arrival in Kumbalari.

It was slow going over the rocky ground and at times we had to dismount and lead our horses. As we climbed higher and higher the air grew much colder and we were glad when evening came and we could make camp, light warming fires and check our maps to see how much further we had to go.

The respective commanders of the Cavalry and the Infantry were Risaldar Jenab Shah and Subadar J. K. Bisht, both of them veterans of many similar expeditions. But for all their experience they were inclined to be warier than usual of the Kumbalaris and Subadar Bisht advised me to put a double guard on the camp, which I did.

Subadar Bisht was worried by what he called 'the smell on the wind'. He knew something about the Kumbalaris and when he spoke of them I saw a glint of what in anyone but a Ghoorka's eyes I might have mistaken for fear. "These are a cunning and treacherous people, sir," he told me as we ate together in my tent, with Jenab Shah, a silent giant, beside us. "They are the inheritors of an ancient evil—an evil which existed before the world was born. In our tongue Kumbalari is called The Kingdom of the Devil. Do not expect them to honour our white flag. They will respect it only while it suits them."

"Fair enough," I said. "But they'll have respect for our numbers and our weapons, I dare say."

"Perhaps." Subadar Bisht looked dubious. "Unless Sharan Kang has convinced them that they are protected by his magic. He is known to draw much power from nameless gods and to have devils at his command."

"Modern guns," I pointed out, "usually prove superior to the most powerful devil, Subadar Bisht."

The Ghoorka looked grave. "Usually, Captain Bastable. And then there is their cunning. They might try to split up our column with various tricks—so they can attack us independently, with more chance of success."

I accepted this. "We'll certainly be on guard against that sort of tactic," I agreed. "But I do not think I fear their magic."

Risaldar Jenab Shah spoke soberly in his deep, rumbling voice. "It is not so much what *we* fear," he said, "but what *they* believe." He smoothed his gleaming black beard. "I agree with the Subadar. We must understand that we are dealing with crazy men—reckless fanatics who will not count the cost of their own lives."

"The Kumbalaris hate us very much," added Subadar Bisht. "They want to fight us. They have not attacked. This I find suspicious. Could it be, sir, that they are letting us enter a trap?"

"Possibly," I replied. "But there again, Subadar Bisht, they may simply be afraid of us—afraid of the power of the British Raj which will send others to punish them most severely if anything should happen to us."

"If they are certain that punishment will not come— if Sharan Kang has convinced them thus—it will not help us." Jenab Shah smiled grimly. "We shall be dead, Captain Bastable."

"If we waited here," Subadar Bisht suggested, "and

let them approach us so that we could hear their words and watch their faces, it would be easier for us to know what to do next."

I agreed with his logic. "Our supplies will last us an extra two days," I said. "We will camp here for two days. If they do not come within that time, we will continue on to Teku Benga."

Both officers were satisfied. We finished our meal and retired to our respective tents.


And so we waited.

On the first day we saw a few riders round the bend in the pass and we made ready to receive them. But they merely watched us for a couple of hours before vanishing. Tension had begun to increase markedly in the camp by the next night.

On the second day one of our scouts rode in to report that over a hundred Kumbalaris had assembled at the far end of the pass and were riding towards us. We assumed a defensive position and continued to wait. When they appeared they were riding slowly and through my field glasses I saw several elaborate horsehair standards. Attached to one of these was a white flag. The standard-bearers rode on both sides of a red and gold litter slung between two ponies. Remembering Subadar Bisht's words of caution, I gave the order for our cavalry to mount. There is hardly any sight more impressive than a hundred and fifty Punjabi Lancers with their lances at the salute. Risaldar Jenab Shah was at my side. I offered him my glasses. He took them and stared through them for some moments. When he lowered them he was frowning. "Sharan Kang seems to be with them," he said, "riding in that litter. Perhaps this is a genuine parley party. But why so many?"

"It could be a show of strength," I said. "But he must have more than a hundred warriors."

"It depends how many have died for religious purposes," Jenab Shah said darkly. He turned in his saddle. "Here is Subadar Bisht. What do you make of this, Bisht?"

The Ghoorka officer said: "Sharan Kang would not ride at their head if they were about to charge. The Priest-Kings of Kumbalari do not fight with their warriors." He spoke with some contempt. "But I warn you, sir, this could be a trick."

I nodded.

Both the Punjabi sowars and the Ghoorka sepoys were plainly eager to come to grips with the Kumbalaris. "You had better remind your men that we are here to talk peace, if possible," I said, "not to fight."

"They will not fight," Jenab Shah said confidently, "until they have orders to do so. Then they will *fight*."

The mass of Kumbalari horsemen drew closer and paused a few hundred feet from our lines. The standard-bearers broke away and, escorting the litter, came up to where I sat my horse at the head of my men.

The red and gold litter was covered by curtains. I looked enquiringly at the impassive faces of the standard-bearers, but they said nothing. And then at last the curtain at the front was parted from within and I was suddenly confronting the High Priest himself. He wore elaborate robes of brocade stitched with dozens of tiny mirrors. On his head was a tall hat of painted leather inlaid with gold and ivory. And beneath the peak of the hat was his wizened old face. The face of a particularly malicious devil.

"Greetings, Sharan Kang," I said. "We are here at the command of the great King-Emperor of Britain. We come to ask why you attack his houses and kill his servants when he has offered no hostility to you."

One of the guides began to interpret, but Sharan Kang waved his hand impatiently. "Sharan Kang speaks English," he said in a strange, high-pitched voice. "As he speaks *all* tongues. For all tongues come from the tongue of the Kumbalari, the First, the Most Ancient."

I must admit I felt a shiver run through me as he

spoke. I could almost believe that he was the powerful sorcerer they claimed him to be.

"Such an ancient people must therefore also be wise." I tried to stare back into those cruel, intelligent eyes. "And a wise people would not anger the King-Emperor."

"A wise people knows that it must protect itself against the wolf," Sharan Kang said, a faint smile curving his lips. "And the British wolf is a singularly rapacious beast, Captain Bastable. It has eaten well in the lands of the south and the west, has it not? Soon it will turn its eyes towards Kumbalari.",

"What you mistake for a wolf is really a lion," I said, trying not to show I was impressed by the fact that he had known my name. "A lion which brings peace, security, justice to those it chooses to protect. A lion which knows that Kumbalari does not need its protection."

The conversation continued in these rather convoluted terms for some time before Sharan Kang grew visibly impatient and said suddenly:

"Why are so many soldiers come to our land?"

"Because you attacked our frontier station and killed our men," I said.

"Because you put your 'frontier station' inside our boundaries." Sharan Kang made a strange gesture in the air. "We are not a greedy people. We have no need to be. We do not hunger for land like the Westerners, for we know that land is not important when a man's soul is capable of ranging the universe. You may come to Teku Benga, where all gods preside, and there I will tell you what you may say to this upstart barbarian lion who dignifies himself with grandiose titles."

"You are willing to discuss a treaty?"

"Yes—in Teku Benga, if you come with no more than six of your men." He gestured, let the curtain fall, and the litter was turned round. The riders began to move back up the valley.

"It is a trick, sir," Bisht remarked at once. "He hopes that in separating you from us he will cut off our army's head and thus make it easier to attack us."

"You could be right, Sabadar Bisht, but you know very well that such a trick would not work. The Ghoorkas are not afraid to fight." I looked back at the sepoys. "Indeed, they seem more than ready to go into battle at this moment."

"We care nothing for death, sir—the clean battle-death. But it is not the prospect of battle which disturbs me. In my bones I feel something worse may happen. I know the Kumbalaris. They are a deeply wicked people. I think what may happen to you in Teku Benga, Captain Bastable."

I laid an affectionate hand on my Sabadar's shoulder. "I am honoured you should feel thus, Sabadar Bisht. But it is my duty to go to Teku Benga. I have my orders. I must settle this matter peacefully if it is at all possible."

"But if you do not return from Teku Benga within a day, sir, we shall advance towards the city. Then, if we are not given full evidence that you are alive and in good health, we shall attack Teku Benga."

"There's nothing wrong with that plan," I agreed.

And so, with Risaldar Jenab Shah and five of his sowars, I rode next morning for Teku Benga and saw at last the walled mountain city into which no stranger had been admitted for a thousand years. Of course I was suspicious of Sharan Kang. Of course I wondered why, after a thousand years, he was willing to let foreigners defile the holy city with their presence. But what could I do? If he said he was willing to discuss a treaty, then I had to believe him.

I was at a loss to imagine how such a city, rearing as it did out of the crags of the Himalayas, had been built. Its crazy spires and domes defied the very laws of gravity. Its crooked walls followed the line of the mountain slopes and many of the buildings looked as if they had been plucked up and perched delicately on slivers of rock which could scarcely support the weight of a man. Many of the roofs and walls were decorated with

complicated carvings of infinitely delicate workman-
ship, set with jewels and precious metals, rare woods,
jade and ivory. Finials curled in on themselves and
curled again. Monstrous stone beasts glared down from
a score of places on the walls. The whole city glit-
tered in the cold light and it did, indeed, seem older
than any architecture I had ever seen or read about.
Yet, for all its richness and its age, Teku Benga struck
me as being a rather seedy sort of place, as if it had
known better days. Perhaps the Kumbalaris had not
built it. Perhaps the race which had built it had mys-
teriously disappeared, as had happened elsewhere, and
the Kumbalaris had merely occupied it.

"Ooof! The stench!" With his handkerchief, Risaldar
Jenab Shah fastidiously wiped his nose. "They must
keep their goats and sheep in their temples and palaces."
   Teku Benga had the smell of a farmyard which had
not been too cleanly kept and the smell grew stronger as
we entered the main gate under the eyes of the glower-
ing guards. Our horses trod irregularly paved streets
caked with dung and other refuse. No women were
present in those streets. All we saw were a few male
children and a number of warriors lounging, with ap-

parent unconcern, by their ponies. We kept going, up the steeply sloping central street, lined with nothing but temples, towards a large square in what I judged to be the middle of the city. The temples themselves were impressively ugly, in a style which a scholar might have called decadent Oriental baroque. Every inch of the buildings was decorated with representations of gods and demons from virtually every mythology in the East. There were mixtures of Hindu and Buddhist decoration, of Moslem and some Christian, of what I took to be Egyptian, Phoenician, Persian, even Greek, and some which were older still; but none of these combinations was at all pleasing to the eye. At least I now understood how it came to be called the Place Where All Gods Preside—though they presided, it seemed to me, in rather uneasy juxtaposition to each other.

"This is distinctly an unhealthy place," said Jenab Shah. "I will be glad to leave it. I should not like to die here, Captain Bastable. I would fear what would happen to my soul."

"I know what you mean. Let us hope Sharan Kang keeps his word."

"I am not sure I heard him give his word, sir," said the Risaldar significantly as we reached the square and reined in our horses. We had arrived outside a huge, ornate building, much larger than the others, but in the same sickening mixture of styles. Domes, minarets, spiralling steeples, lattice-walls, pagoda-like terraced roofs, carved pillars, serpent finials, fabulous monsters grinning or growling from every corner, tigers and elephants standing guard at every doorway. The building was predominantly coloured green and saffron, but there was red and blue and orange and gold and some of the roofs were overlaid with gold- or silver-leaf. It seemed the oldest temple of them all. Behind all this was the blue Himalayan sky in which grey and white clouds boiled. It was a sight unlike anything I had ever previously experienced. It filled me with a sense of deep foreboding as if I were in the presence of something not built by human hands at all.

Slowly, from all the many doorways, saffron-robed priests began to emerge and stand stock still, watching us from the steps and galleries of the building which was Temple or Palace, or both, I could not decide.

These priests looked little different from the warriors we had seen earlier and they were certainly no cleaner. It occurred to me that if the Kumbalaris disdained land, then they disliked water even more. I remarked on this to Risaldar Jenab Shah who flung back his great turbanned head and laughed heartily—an action which caused the priests to frown at us in hatred and disgust. These priests were not shaven-headed, like most priests who wore the saffron robe. These had long hair hanging down their faces in many greasy braids and some had moustaches or beards which were plaited in a similar fashion. They were a sinister, unsavoury lot. Not a few had belts or cummerbunds into which were stuck scabbarded swords.

We waited and they watched us. We returned their gaze, trying to appear much less concerned than we felt. Our horses moved uneasily under us and tossed their manes, snorting as if the stink of the city was too much, even for them.

Then at last, borne by four priests, the golden litter appeared from what must have been the main entrance of the temple. The curtains were parted and there sat Sharan Kang.

He was grinning.

"I am here, Sharan Kang," I began, "to listen to anything you wish to tell me concerning your raids on our frontier stations and to discuss the terms of a treaty which will let us live together in peace."

Sharan Kang's grin did not falter, but I'm afraid my voice did a little as I stared into that wrinkled, evil face. I had never before felt convinced that I was in the presence of pure evil, but I did at that moment.

After a moment he spoke. "I hear your words and

must consider them. Meanwhile you will be guests here—" he gestured behind him—"here at the Temple of the Future Buddha which is also my palace. The oldest of all these ancient buildings."

A little nervously we dismounted. The four priests picked up Sharan Kang's litter and bore it back inside. We followed. The interior was heavy with incense and poorly lighted by sputtering bowls of flaming oil suspended from chains fixed to the ceiling. There were no representations of the Buddha here, however, and I supposed that this was because the 'future Buddha' had not yet been born. We followed the litter through a system of corridors, so complicated as to seem like a maze, until we reached a smallish chamber in which food had been laid on a low table surrounded by cushions. Here the litter was lowered and the attendant priests retired, apparently leaving us alone with Sharan Kang. He gestured for us to seat ourselves on the cushions, which we did.

"You must eat and drink," intoned Sharan Kang, "and then we shall all feel more like talking."

After washing our hands in the silver bowls of warm water and drying them on the silken towels, we reached, rather reluctantly, towards the food. Sharan Kang helped himself to the same dishes and began to eat heartily, which was something of a relief to us. When we tasted the food we were glad that it did not seem poisoned, for it was delicious.

I complimented the High Priest sincerely on his hospitality and he accepted this graciously enough. He was beginning to seem a much less sinister figure. In fact I was almost beginning to like him.

"It is unusual," I said, "to have a Temple which is also a Palace—and with such a strange name, too."

"The High Priests of Kumbalari," said Sharan Kang smiling, "are also gods, so they must live in a temple. And since the Future Buddha is not yet here to take up residence, what better place than this temple?"

31

"They must have been waiting a long time for him to come. How old is this building?"

"Some parts of it are little more than fifteen hundred or two thousand years old. Other parts are perhaps three to five thousand years old. The earliest parts are much, much older than that."

I did not believe him, of course, but accepted what he said as a typical oriental exaggeration. "And have the Kumbalaris lived here all that time?" I asked politely.

"They have lived here a long, long time. Before that there were—other beings . . ."

A look almost of fear came into his eyes and he smiled quickly. "Is the food to your taste?"

"It is very rich," I said. I felt an emotion of fondness for him, as I might have felt as a child to a kindly uncle. I looked at the others. And that was when I became suspicious, for all had stupid, vacant grins on their faces. And I was feeling drowsy! I shook my head, trying to clear it. I got unsteadily to my feet. I shook Risaldar Jenab Shah's shoulder. "Are you all right, Risaldar?"

He looked up at me and laughed, then nodded sagely as if I had made some particularly wise pronouncement.

Now I understood why I had felt so well-disposed towards the cunning old High Priest.

"You have drugged us, Sharan Kang! Why? You think any concessions we make in this state will be honoured when we realise what has been done to us? Or do you plan to mesmerise us—make us give orders to our men which will lead them into a trap."

Sharan Kang's eyes were hard. "Sit down, captain. I have not drugged you. I ate the food you ate. Am I drugged?"

"Possibly . . ." I staggered and had to force my legs to support me. The room had begun to spin. "If you are used to the drug and we are not. What is it? Opium?"

Sharan Kang laughed. "Opium! Opium! Why should it be, Captain Bastable? If you are feeling sleepy it is only because you have eaten so much of the rich food of Kumbalari. You have been living on the simpler diet of a soldier. Why not sleep for a while and . . . ?"

My mouth was dry and my eyes were watering. Sharan Kang, murmuring softly, seemed to sway before me like a cobra about to strike. Cursing him I unbuttoned my holster and drew out my revolver.

Instantly a dozen of the priests appeared, their curved swords at the ready. I tried to aim at Sharan Kang.

"Come closer and he dies," I said thickly.

I was not sure that they understood the words, but they gathered my meaning.

"Sharan Kang." My own voice seemed to come from a great distance away. "My men will march on Teku Benga tomorrow. If I do not appear before them, alive and well, they will attack your city and they will destroy it and all who live in it."

Sharan Kang only smiled. "Of course you will be alive and well, captain. Moreover you will see things in an improved perspective, I am sure."

"My God! You'll not mesmerise me! I'm an English officer—not one of your ignorant followers!"

"Please rest, captain. In the morning . . ."

From the corner of my eye I caught a movement. Two more priests were rushing me from behind. I turned and fired. One went down. The other closed with me, trying to wrench the gun from my grasp. I fired it and blew a great hole in him. With a cry he released my wrist and fell writhing to the ground. Now the Punjabis were beside me, their own pistols drawn, doing their best to support each other, for all were as badly drugged as was I. Jenab Shah said with difficulty: "We must try to reach fresh air, captain. It might help. And if we can get to our horses, we may escape . . ."

"You'll be fools to leave this room," said Sharan Kang evenly. "Even we do not know every part of the maze which is the Temple of the Future Buddha. Some say that sections of it do not even exist in our own time . . ."

"Be silent!" I ordered, covering him again with my pistol. "I'll not listen further to your lies."

We began to back away from Sharan Kang and his remaining priests, our revolvers at the ready as we looked around for the entrance through which we had come. But all entrances looked alike. At last we chose one and staggered through it, finding ourselves in almost total blackness.

As we blundered about, seeking a door which would lead us outside, I wondered again at the reasons for Sharan Kang's drugging us. I shall never know what his exact plans were, however.

Suddenly one of our men gave a yell and fired into the darkness. At first I saw nothing but a blank wall. Then two or three priests came running at us from thin air, apparently unarmed—but impervious to the man's bullets.

"Stop firing!" I rasped, convinced that this was an optical illusion. "Follow me!" I stumbled down a flight of steps, pushed through an awning, found myself in another chamber laid out with food—but not the same chamber in which we had eaten. I hesitated. Was I already in the grip of a drugged dream? I crossed the room, knocking over a small stool as I passed the table, and dashed back a series of silk curtains until I discovered an exit. With my men behind me I passed through the archway, striking my shoulders painfully as I weaved from side to side of the corridor. Another flight of steps. Another chamber almost exactly like the first, laid out with food. Another exit and still another flight of steps leading downward. A passage.

I don't know for how long this useless stumbling about went on, but it felt like an eternity. We were completely lost and our only consolation was that our enemies seemed to have given up their pursuit. We were deep in an unlit part of the Temple of the Future Buddha. There was no smell of incense here—only cold, stale air. Everything I touched was cold; carved from rock and studded with raw jewels and metal, every inch of the walls seemed covered in gargoyles. Sometimes my fingers would trace part of a carving and then recoil in horror at the vision which was conjured up.

The drug was still in us, but the strenuous exercise had diminished part of its effect. My head was beginning to clear when at last I paused, panting, and tried to review our position.

"I think we are in an unused part of the Temple," I said, "and a long way below the level of the street, judging by all those steps we went down. I wonder why they haven't followed us. If we wait here for a little while and then try to make our way back undetected, we stand a chance of reaching our men and warning them of Sharan Kang's treachery. Any other ideas, Risaldar?"

There was silence.

I peered into the darkness. "Risaldar?"

No reply.

I reached into my pocket and took out a box of matches. I lit one.

All I saw were the horrid carvings—infinitely more disgusting than those in the upper parts of the building. They seemed both inhuman and unbelievably ancient. I could understand now why we had not been followed. I dropped the match with a gasp. Where were my men?

I risked calling out. "Risaldar? Jenab Shah?"

Still silence.

I shuddered, beginning to believe in everything I had been told about Sharan Kang's power. I found myself stumbling forward, trying to run, falling on the stone and picking myself up, running again, insane with terror, until, completely exhausted, I fell to the deathly cold floor of the Temple of the Future Buddha.

I might have passed out for a short while, but the next thing I remember was a peculiar noise—unmistakeably

the sound of distant, tinkling laughter. Sharan Kang?
No.

I reached out, trying to touch the walls. I found only
empty space on both sides of me. I had left the corridor,
I supposed, and entered a chamber. I shivered. Again
that peculiar, tinkling laughter.

And then I saw a tiny light ahead of me. I got up
and began to move towards it, but it must have been a
very long way away, for it grew no larger.

I stopped.

Then the light began to move towards *me!*

And as it came closer, the sound of the unearthly
laughter grew louder until I was forced to holster my
pistol and cover my ears. The light intensified. I
squeezed my eyes shut in pain. The ground beneath
my feet began to sway. An earthquake?

I risked opening my eyes for a moment and through
the blinding white light got an impression of more inhuman carvings, or strange, complicated things which
might have been machines built by the ancient Hindu
gods.

And then the floor seemed to give way beneath me
and I was plunging downwards, was caught by a whirl-
wind and hurled upward, was tossed head over heels,
dashed from side to side, hurled downward again, until
my senses left me altogether, save for that sensation of
bitter, bitter cold.

Then I felt nothing, not even the cold. I became convinced that I was dead, slain by a force which had
lurked below the Temple since the beginnings of Time
and which even Sharan Kang, Master Sorcerer of Teku
Benga, had been afraid to face.

Then I ceased to think at all.

## CHAPTER III

### The Shadow from the Sky

CONSCIOUSNESS RETURNED FIRST as a series of vague impressions: armies, consisting of millions of men, marching against a background of grey and white trees; black flames burning; a young girl in a white dress, her body pierced by dozens of long arrows. There were many images of that sort and slowly they became stronger and the colours grew richer and richer. I became aware of my own body. It was colder than ice—colder even than it had been before I had passed out. And yet, oddly, I felt no discomfort. I felt nothing—I just *knew* that I was cold.

I tried to move the fingers on my right hand (I could still see nothing) and thought that perhaps the index finger rose a fraction.

The images in my head grew more horrific. Corpses filled my skull—brutally maimed corpses. Dying children stretched out their hands to me for help. Bestial soldiers in colourless uniforms raped women. And everywhere there was fire, black smoke, collapsing buildings. I had to escape those images and I made a great effort to move my arm.

At last the arm began to bend, but it was amazingly stiff. And as it bent pain flooded through me so that I cried out—a strange, grating noise. My eyes sprang open and at first I saw nothing but a milky haze. I moved my neck. Again the sickening pain. But the images were beginning to fade. I bent my leg and gasped. Suddenly fire seemed to fill me, melting the ice which had frozen my blood. I began to shake all over, but the pain diminished. And now I saw that I lay on my back staring up at the blue sky. I seemed to be at the bottom of a pit, for there were steep walls on every side.

After a very long time I was able to sit upright and inspect my surroundings. I *was* in a pit of sorts—but a man-made pit, for the shaft was of carved stone. The carvings were similar to those I had glimpsed fleetingly before I collapsed. In the daylight they did not look quite so daunting, but they were ugly things nonetheless.

I smiled at my fears. Plainly there had been an earthquake and it had shaken down the Temple of the Future Buddha. The other things I had seen had been caused by the action of the drug on my frightened brain. Somehow I had escaped the worst of the earthquake and was relatively unhurt. I doubted if Sharan Kang and his people had been so lucky, but I had best go warily until I knew for certain that they were not waiting for me up above. Probably poor Risaldar Jenab Shah and the sowars had been killed in the catacombs. But at least Nature had done the work I had been commissioned to do—the earthquake would have 'pacified' even Sharan Kang. Even if he were not dead, he would now be discredited, for those of his people still alive would see the earthquake as a sign from the gods.

I got to my feet, staring at my hands. They were caked with dust that was not only thick but which seemed to have been there for ages. And my clothes were in rags. As I slapped at the dust, bits of cloth fell away. I fingered my jacket. The fabric seemed to have *rotted!* I was momentarily disturbed, but then reasoned that they had been affected by the action of some peculiar gas which filled the deeper chambers of the temple —a gas which had perhaps combined with the drug to make me suffer those strange hallucinations.

When I felt in slightly better shape, I began, as cautiously as I could, to try to make my way up to the top of the pit, which was some thirty feet above my head. I was extremely weak and frightfully stiff and the rock was soft, often breaking away as I tested it for a foothold. But by using the gargoyles as steps, I slowly managed to clamber to the top of the pit, haul myself over the edge and peer cautiously around me.

There was no sign of Sharan Kang or his men. Indeed, there was no sign of life at all. Everywhere I looked I saw ruins. Not a single building in Teku Benga had escaped the earthquake. Many of the temples seemed to have disappeared altogether.

I stood up and began to walk over the cracked remains of the pavements.

And then I stopped suddenly and, for the first time since I had awakened, I realised that there was something I could not rationalise.

There were no corpses—which might have been expected if the earthquake had occurred the previous night, as I thought. But perhaps the people had managed to escape the city. I could accept that.

What brought me up short was not that the pavements were cracked—*but that weeds grew in profusion between the cracks!*

And now that I looked, there were creepers, tiny mountain flowers, patches of heather growing everywhere on the ruins. These ruins were *old.* It had been years since anyone had occupied them!

I licked my lips and tried to pull myself together. Perhaps I was not in Teku Benga at all? Perhaps I had been carried from Sharan Kang's city and left to die among the ruins of another city?

But this was plainly Teku Benga. I recognised the ruins of several buildings. And there was hardly another city *like* Teku Benga, even in the mysterious Himalayas.

Besides, I recognised the surrounding mountains, the distant pass which led up to what had been the city wall. And it was obvious that I stood in the ruins of the central square in which the Temple of the Future Buddha had been erected.

Again I experienced a dreadful shiver of fear. Again I glanced down at my dust-caked body, at my rotting clothes, at the weeds beneath my split boots, at all the evidence—evidence which mocked my sanity—evidence to show that not hours but *years* had passed since I had sought to escape the trap which Sharan Kang had set for me!

Could I still be dreaming? I asked myself. But if this were a dream, it was unlike anything I had ever dreamed before. And one can always tell a dream from reality, no matter how sharp and coherent a dream it is. (That is what I felt then, but now I wonder, I wonder. . . .)

I seated myself on a slab of broken masonry and tried to think. How was it possible than I could still be alive? At least two years must have passed since the earthquake—if earthquake it were—and while my clothes had been subjected to the normal processes of Time, my flesh was unaffected. Could the gas I suspected as having caused the rot have actually preserved me? It was the only explanation—and a wild enough one, at that. It would take a clever scientist to investigate the matter. I wasn't up to it. Now my job was to get back to civilisation, contact my regiment and find out what had been going on since I had lost consciousness.

As I clambered over the ruins I tried to force the astounding thoughts from my brain and concentrate on my immediate problem. But it was difficult and I still could not rid myself entirely of the idea that I had gone quite mad.

Eventually I reached the crumbling walls and hauled my aching body over them. Reaching the top I looked down the other side, seeking the road which had been there. But it was gone. In its place was a yawning chasm, as if the rock had cracked wide open and the part of the mountain on which the city had stood had moved at least a hundred feet away from the rest. There was absolutely no way of crossing to the other side. I began to laugh—a harsh, exhausted cackle—and then was seized by a series of dry, racking sobs. Somehow Fate had spared my life, only to present me with the prospect of a lingering death as I slowly starved on this lifeless mountain.

Wearily, I lay down my head and must have slept a natural sleep for an hour or two, for when I awoke the sun was lower in the sky. It was about three o'clock in the afternoon.

I dragged myself to my feet, turned and began to move back through the ruins. I would try to get to the other side of the city and see if there were any other means of climbing down the mountain.

All around me were the snow-capped flanks of the Himalayas: impassive, uncaring. And above me was the pale blue sky in which not even a hawk flew. It was almost as if I were the last creature alive in the world.

I stopped myself from continuing this line of thought, for I knew that madness would be the result if I did begin to reason in that way.

When I did eventually reach the far side of the city hopelessness once again consumed me, for on all the remaining quarters there were sheer cliffs going down several hundred feet at least. That was doubtless the reason for locating the city here in the first place. There was only one approach—or had been—and it meant that Teku Benga was safe from anything but a frontal attack. I shrugged in despair and began to wonder which of the plants might be edible. Not that I was hungry at that moment. I smiled bitterly. Why should I be, if I had remained alive for at least two years? The joke made me laugh. It was a crazy laugh. I stopped myself. The sun was beginning to set and the air had grown cold. At length I crawled into a shelter formed by two slabs of masonry and fell once more into a deep, dreamless sleep.

It was dawn when I next awoke. I felt a new confidence and I had devised a plan of sorts. My leather belt and shoulder strap had been unaffected by time and though slightly cracked were still strong. I would search the ruins until I found more leather. Somewhere there must still be storechests, even the remains of the Kumbalari warriors who had died in the earthquake. I would devote what remained of my energy to discovering enough leather out of which I might plait a rope. With a rope I could try to get down the mountain. And if I died in the attempt, well, it would be no worse than the alternative means of dying which were presented to me.

I spent the next several hours clambering in and out of the ruins, discovering first a skeleton still dressed in the furs, iron and leather of a Kumbalari soldier. Around his waist was wound quite a good length of leather cord. I tested it and it was still strong. My spirits lifting, I continued to search.

I was crouching in the ruins of one of the temples, trying to drag out another skeleton, when I first heard the sound. At first I thought it was a noise made by the bones scraping on the rock, but it was too soft. Then I wondered if I were, after all, not alone in the ruins. Could I be hearing the purr of a tiger? No—though that was more like the sound. I stopped tugging at the skeleton and cocked my head, trying to listen harder. A drum, perhaps? A drumbeat echoing through the mountains? It could be fifty miles away, however. I crawled back through the gap and as I did so a shadow began to spread across the rubble before me. A huge, black shadow which might have been that of an enormous bird, save that it was long, regular in shape and curved.

Again I doubted my own sanity and in some trepidation I forced myself to look upward.

I gasped in astonishment. This was no bird, but a gigantic, cigar-shaped balloon! And yet it was like no balloon I had ever seen, for its envelope seemed rigid—constructed of some silvery metal—and attached to this envelope (not swinging from it by ropes) was a gondola almost the length of the balloon itself.

What astonished me even more was the slogan, inscribed in huge lettering on the hull:

ROYAL INDIAN AIR SERVICE

From its stern projected four triangular 'wings' which resembled nothing so much as the flat tail-fins of a whale. And painted on each of these in shining red, white and blue was a large Union Jack.

For a moment I could only stare at the flying monster in incredulous wonderment. And then I began to leap about the ruins, waving and yelling for all I was worth!

# CHAPTER IV

## An Amateur Archaeologist

I MUST HAVE seemed a pretty strange sight myself, with my filthy body clad in rotting clothes, dancing and roaring like a madman among the ruins of that ancient city, just as if I were some castaway of old who had at last caught sight of the schooner which could save him. But it did not look as if this schooner of the air had seen me. Imperturbably it sailed on, heading towards the distant northern mountains, its four great engines thumping out their smooth, regular beat, turning the massive, whirling screws which apparently propelled the vessel.

It passed over the ruins and seemed to be continuing on its course, as unaware of me as it might have been of a fly settling on its side.

The engines stopped. I waited tensely. What would the balloon do next? It was still moving forward, carried on by its own momentum.

When the engines started again their sound was more high-pitched. I sank down in despair. Possibly the flyers (assuming there *were* men in the monster) had thought they had seen something but then decided it was not worth stopping to investigate. A tremor ran through the great silver bulk and then, very slowly, it began to drift backwards—back to where I sat panting and anxious. The screws had been put into reverse, rather as the screws on a steamer are reversed.

Again I leapt up, my face splitting into a huge grin. I was to be saved—even if it were by the strangest flying machine ever invented.

Soon the great bulk—the size of a small steamer itself—was over my head, blotting out the sky. Half-crazy with joy, I continued to wave. I heard distant shouts from above but could not distinguish the words. A siren started to blow, but I took this to be a greeting, like a ship's whistle.

Then, suddenly, something dropped from the ship. I was struck savagely in the face and smashed backwards against the rock. I gasped for breath, unable to understand the reason for the attack or, for that matter, what missile had been used.

Blinking, I sat up and peered around me. For yards in all directions the ruins glistened wetly—and there were several huge puddles now in evidence. I was soaked through. Was this some rather bad joke at my expense—their way of telling me that I needed a bath? It seemed unlikely. Shakily, I got up, half-expecting the airship to send down another mass of water.

But then I realised that the vessel was sinking rapidly towards the ruins, looming low in the sky, still sounding its siren. It was lucky for me it had not carried sand as ballast—for ballast was what that water had been! Much lightened, the balloon was able to come to my assistance more quickly.

Soon it was little more than twenty feet above me. I stared hard at the slogan on its side, at the Union Jacks on its tail fins. There was no question of its reality. I had once seen an airship flown by Mr Santos-Dumont, but it had been a crude affair compared with this giant. There had been a great deal of progress in the last couple of years, I decided.

Now a circular hatch was opened in the bottom of the metal gondola and amused British faces peered over the lip.

"Sorry about the bath, old son," called one in familiar Cockney tones, "but we did try to warn you. Understand English?"

"I *am* English!" I croaked.

"Blimey! Hang on a minute." The face disappeared.

"All right," said the face, reappearing. "Stand clear there."

I stepped back nervously, expecting another drenching, but this time a rope ladder snaked down from the hatch. I ran forward and grabbed it in relief but as soon as my hand clasped the first run I heard a yell from overhead:

"Not yet! Not yet! Oh, Murphy, the idiot! The—"

I missed the rest of the oath for I was being dragged over the rocks until I managed to let go of the rung and fall flat on my face. The flying machine had yawed round a fraction in the sky—a fraction being a good few feet—and laid me low for a second time! I got up and did not attempt to grab the rope ladder again.

"We'll come down," shouted the face. "Stay where you are."

Soon two smartly dressed men clambered from the hatch and began to descend the ladder. They were dressed in white uniforms very similar to those worn by sailors in the tropics, though their jackets and trousers were edged with broad bands of light blue and I did not recognise the insignia on their sleeves. I admired the casual skill and speed with which they climbed down the swaying ladder, paying out a rope which led upwards into the ship. When they were a few rungs above me they tossed me a rope.

"Easy now, old son," called the man who had originally addressed me. "Tie this round you—under your arms —and we'll take you up! Understand?"

"I understand." Swiftly I obeyed his instructions.

"Are you secure?" called the man.

I nodded and took a good grip on the rope.

The sky 'sailor' signalled to an unseen shipmate. "Haul away, Bert!"

I heard the whine of a motor and then I was being dragged upwards. At first I began to spin wildly round and round and felt appallingly sick and dizzy until one of the men on the ladder leaned out and caught my leg, steadying my ascent.

After what must have been a minute but which seemed like an hour I was tugged over the side of the hatch and found myself in a circular chamber about twelve feet in diameter and about eight feet high. The chamber was made entirely of metal and rather resembled a gun-turret in a modern ironclad. The small engine-driven winch which had been the means of bringing me up was now switched off by another uniformed man, doubtless 'Bert'. The other two clambered aboard, gathered in the rope ladder in an expert way, and shut the hatch with a clang, bolting it tight.

There was one other man in the chamber, standing near an oval-shaped door. He, too, was dressed in 'whites', but wore a solar topee and had major's pips on the epaulettes of his shirt. He was a smallish man with a sharp, vulpine face, a neat little black moustache which he was smoothing with the end of his swagger-stick as he peered at me, poker-faced.

After a pause, while his large, dark eyes took in my appearance from head to toe, he said: "Welcome aboard, English are you?"

I finished removing the rope from under my arms and saluted. "Yes, sir. Captain Oswald Bastable, sir."

"Army, eh? Bit odd, eh? I'm Major Powell, Royal Indian Air Police—as you've probably noticed, what? This is the patrol ship *Pericles*." He scratched his long nose with the edge of his stick. "Amazin'—amazin'. Well, we'll talk later. Sick Bay for you first, I'd say, what?"

He opened the oval door and stood aside while the two men helped me through.

I now found myself in a long passageway, blank on one side but with large portholes on the other. Through the portholes I could see the ruins of Teku Benga slowly falling away below us. At the end of the passage was another door and, beyond the door, a corner into a shorter passage on both sides of which were ranged more doors bearing various signs. One of the signs was SICK BAY.

There were eight beds inside, none of which was occupied. There were all the facilities of a modern hospital, including several gadgets at whose use I could not begin to guess. I was allowed to undress behind a screen and take a long bath in the tub I found there. Feeling much better, I got into the pair of pyjamas (also white and sky blue) provided and made my way to the bed which had been prepared at the far end of the room.

I was in something of a trance, I must admit. It was difficult to remember that I was in a room which at this moment was probably floating several hundred feet or more above the mountains of the Himalayas. Occasionally there was a slight motion from side to side or the odd bump, such as one might feel on a train, and, in fact, it did rather feel as if I were on a train—a rather luxurious first class express, perhaps.

After a few minutes the ship's doctor entered the room and had a few words with the orderly who was folding up the screens. The doctor was a youngish man with a great round head and a shock of red hair. When he spoke it was in a soft Scottish accent.

"Captain Bastable is it?"

"That's right, doctor. I'm all right, I think. In my body, at any rate."

"Your body? What d'you think's wrong with your head?"

"Frankly, sir, I think I'm probably dreaming."

"That's what *we* thought when you were first spotted. How on earth did you manage to get up into those ruins? I thought it was impossible." As he spoke he checked my pulse, looked at my eyes and did the usual things doctors do to you when they can't find anything specifically wrong.

"I'm not sure you'd believe me, doctor, if I told you I rode up on horseback," I said.

He gave a peculiar laugh and stuck a thermometer into my mouth. "No, I don't think I would! Rode up! Ha!"

"Well," I said cautiously, after he had removed the thermometer, "I did ride up there."

"Aye." Plainly he didn't believe me. "Possibly you think you did. And the horse jumped that chasm, did it?"

"There wasn't a chasm there when I went there."

"No chasm—?" He laughed aloud. "My stars! No chasm! There's always been a chasm there—for a damned long time, at any rate. That's why we were flying over the ruins. The only way to reach them is by airship. Major Powell's a bit of an amateur archaeologist. He's got permission to reconnoitre this area with a view to exploring Teku Benga some time. He knows more about the lost civilisations of the Himalayas than anyone. He's a scholar, our Major Powell."

"I'd hardly count Kumbalari as a *lost* civilisation," I said. "Not in the strict sense. That earthquake could only have happened a couple of years ago, surely. That's when I went there."

"Two years ago? You've been in that God-forsaken place for two years? You poor fellow. But you're remarkably fit on it, I'll say that." He frowned suddenly. "Earthquake? I haven't heard of an earthquake in Teku Benga. Mind you . . ."

"There hasn't been an earthquake in Teku Benga in living memory." It was the sharp, precise voice of Major Powell who had come in as we talked. He looked at me with a certain wary curiosity. "And I very much doubt that anyone could live there for two years. There's nothing to eat, for one thing. On the other hand, there's no other explanation as to how you got there—unless a private expedition I haven't heard about *flew* there two years ago."

It was my turn to smile. "Hardly likely, sir. No ship of this kind existed two years ago. In fact, it's remarkable how . . ."

"I think you had better check him up here, Jim," said Major Powell tapping his head with his stick. "The poor chap's lost all sense of time—or something. What was the date when you left for Teku Benga, Captain Bastable?"

"June twenty-fifth, sir."

"Um. And what year?"

"Why, 1902, sir."

The doctor and the major stared at each other in some concern.

"That's when the earthquake happened, all right," Major Powell said quietly. "1902. Almost everyone killed. And there *were* some English soldiers there. . . . Oh, by God! This is ridiculous!" He returned his attention to me. "You are in a serious condition, young man. I wouldn't call it amnesia—but some sort of false memory. Mind playing you tricks, um? Maybe you've read a lot of history, eh, like me? Perhaps you're an amateur archaeologist, too? Well, I expect we can soon cure you and learn what really happened."

"What's so odd about my story, major?"

"Well, for one thing, old chap, you're a bit too well-preserved to have gone up to Teku Benga in 1902. That was over seventy years ago. This is July the fifteenth. The year, I'm afraid, is 1973. A.D., of course. Does that ring a bell?"

I shook my head. "Sorry, major. But I'll agree with you on one thing. I'm obviously completely insane."

"Let's hope it's not permanent," smiled the doctor. "Probably been reading a bit too much H. G. Wells, eh?"


## CHAPTER V

### My First Sight of Utopia


EVIDENTLY OUT OF a mistaken sense of kindness, both the doctor and Major Powell left me alone. I had received a hypodermic injection containing some kind of drug which made me drowsy, but I could not sleep. I had become totally convinced now that some peculiar force in the catacombs of the Temple of the Future Buddha had propelled me through Time. I *knew* that it was true. I *knew* that I was not mad. Indeed, if I were mad, then there would be little point in fighting such a detailed and consistent delusion—I might just as well accept it. But now I wanted more information about the world into which I had been plunged. I wanted to discuss the possibilities with the doctor and the major. I wanted to know if there were any evidence of such a thing having happened before—any unexplained reports of men who claimed to have come from another age. At this thought I became depressed. Doubtless there *were* other accounts. And doubtless, too, those men had been considered mad and committed to lunatic asylums, or charlatans and committed to prison. If I were to remain free to see more of this world of the Future, to discover, if I could, a means of returning to my own time, then it would not do for me to make too strong a claim for the truth. It would be better for me to affect amnesia. That they would understand better. And if they could invent an explanation as to how I came to be in the ruins of Teku Benga seventy years after the last man had been able to set foot there, then good luck to them!

Feeling much happier about the whole thing, having made my decision, I settled back in the pillows and fell into a doze.

"The ship's about to land, sir."

It was the voice of the orderly which wakened me from my trance. I struggled up in the bed, but he put a restraining hand on me. "Don't worry, sir. Just lie back and enjoy the ride. We're transferring you to the hospital as soon as we're safely moored. Just wanted to let you know."

"Thanks," I said weakly.

"You must have been through it, sir," said the orderly

sympathetically. "Mountain climbing is a tricky business in that sort of country."

"Who told you I'd been mountain climbing?"

He was confused. "Well, nobody, sir. We just thought . . . Well, it was the obvious explanation."

"The obvious explanation? Yes, why not? Thank you again, orderly."

He frowned as he turned away. "Don't mention it, sir."

A little while later they began to remove the bolts which had fixed the bed to the deck. I had hardly been aware—save for a slight sinking sensation and a few tremors—that the ship had landed. I was wheeled along the corridors until we reached what I guessed to be the middle of the ship. Here huge folding doors had been lowered to form steps to the ground and a ramp had been laid over the steps to make it possible to wheel my bed down.

We emerged into clear, warm air and the bed bumped a trifle as it was wheeled over flattened grass to what was plainly a hospital van, for it had large red crosses painted on its white sides. The van was motorised, by the look of it. There were no horses in evidence. Glancing around me I received my second shock of pure astonishment at the sight which now met my gaze. Dotted about a vast field were a number of towers, smaller than, but strongly resembling, the Eiffel Tower in Paris. About half of these towers were in use—great pyramids of steel girders to which were moored the best part of a dozen airships, most of which were considerably larger than the giant in which I had been brought! It was obvious that not all the flying monsters were military vessels. Some were commercial, having the names of their lines painted on their sides and decorated rather more elaborately than, for instance, the *Pericles*.

The doctor came up alongside as my bed bumped across the grass. "How are you feeling?"

"Better, thanks. Where are we?"

"Don't you recognise it? It's Katmandu. Our head-quarters are here."

Katmandu! The last time I had seen the city it had been very distinctly an Eastern capital with architecture in the age-old style of these parts. But now in the distance, beyond the great mooring towers, I could see tall white buildings rising up and up, storey upon storey, so that it seemed they almost touched the clouds. Certainly there were Nepalese buildings, too, but these were completely dwarfed by the soaring white piles. I noticed something else before I was lifted into the motor-van—a long ribbon of steel, raised on a series of grey pillars, which stretched away from the city and disappeared over the horizon.

"And what is that?" I asked the doctor.

He looked puzzled. "What? The monorail? Why, just a monorail, of course."

"You mean a train runs along that single track?"

"Exactly." He paused as he got into the van with me and the doors closed with a soft hiss of air. "You know, Bastable, your surprise is damned convincing. I wish I knew what was really wrong with you."

I decided to propose my lie. "Could it be amnesia, doctor?" There was a soft bump as the van began to move. But I did not hear the familiar clatter of an internal-combustion engine. "What's powering this thing?"

"What did you expect? It's steam, of course. This is an ordinary Stanley flash-fired steamer van."

"Not a petrol engine?"

"I should hope not! Primitive things. The steam motor is infinitely more efficient. You must know all this, Bastable. I'm not saying you're deliberately trying to deceive me, but . . ."

"I think you'd better assume that I've forgotten everything but my name, doctor. All the rest is probably a delusion I went through. Something brought on by exposure and despair at ever being rescued. You'll probably find I'm the survivor of a mountain climbing expedition which disappeared some time ago."

"Yes." He spoke in some relief. "I thought it might be mountain climbing. You can't remember going up? What the names of the others were—things like that?"

"Afraid not."

"Well," he said, satisfied, "we're beginning to make a start, at any rate."

Eventually the van stopped and I was wheeled out again, this time onto a raised loading platform plainly designed for the purpose. Through a pair of doors (which opened apparently without human agency) and into a clean, bright corridor until I reached a room which was equally clean and bright—and featureless.

"Here we are," said the doctor.

"And here is?"

"The Churchill Hospital—named after the late Viceroy, Lord Winston. Did a lot for India, did Churchill."

"Is that the Churchill who wrote the books? The war reports? The chap who charged with the 21st Lancers at Omdurman in '98?"

"I think so. That was early on in his career. You certainly know your history!"

"Well, he must have settled down a lot," I smiled, "to have become the Viceroy of India!"

The doctor offered me another strange look. "Aye, well, Captain Bastable. You'll only be in Katmandu a day or two—until the hospital train leaves for Calcutta. I think you need a specialist in—amnesia. The nearest is at Calcutta."

I held my tongue. I was about to wonder, aloud, if Calcutta had changed as much as Katmandu.

"And it's peaceful, these days," I said, "around here, is it?"

"Peaceful? I should hope so. Oh, there's the odd bit of trouble from extreme nationalist groups from time to time, but nothing serious. There haven't been any *wars* for, what, a hundred years."

"My amnesia *is* bad," I said, smiling.

He stood awkwardly at my bedside. "Aye—well . . . Ah!" He exclaimed in relief. "Here's your nurse. Cheerio,

Bastable. Keep your spirits up. I'll just—" He took the nurse by her elbow and steered her outside, closing the door.

I would not be a man, with a man's instincts, if I did not admit I had been both surprised and delighted at the appearance of my nurse. It had only been a glimpse, but it showed me just how much things had changed since 1902. The nurse's uniform had been starched white and blue, with a stiff cap on her neatly pinned auburn hair. A fairly ordinary nurse's uniform, save for one thing: her skirt was at least *twelve inches* clear of the floor and revealed the prettiest pair of calves, the neatest set of ankles I had ever seen off the stage of The Empire, Leicester Square! It certainly gave the nurse greater freedom of movement and was, essentially, practical. I wondered if all women were dressed in this practical and attractive way. If so, I could see unexpected pleasures arising from my unwitting trip into the Future!

I think I alarmed my nurse when she returned, for I was both embarrassed and fascinated by her appearance. It was hard to see her as an ordinary, decent —indeed, rather prim—young woman when she was, in the terms of my own day, dressed like a ballet girl! I think I must have been blushing rather noticeably, for the first thing she did was to take my pulse.

A little while later, Major Powell came in and drew up the steel-framed chair beside the bed. "Well, how are you feeling now, old chap?"

"Much better," I said. "I think I must have amnesia." (I had repeated this line so frequently it was almost as if I were trying to convince myself!)

"So the doc was saying. More like it. And you remember something about a mountain climbing expedition, do you?"

"I think I do remember going up the mountain," I said truthfully.

"Splendid! It won't take long for your memory to

come back. Mind you, I'm damned interested in what you were saying. It would have been good luck for me if you really had come from 1902, what?"

I smiled weakly. "Why is that, major?"

"Would have helped my researches. I'm particularly interested in Teku Benga. It's an enigma, you know, architecturally and historically speaking. It has no right to be there, by all logic. And the aerial photographs we've got of it show a mixture of architectural styles which suggests that it was for a time a meeting place for all the world's cultures. Hard to credit, I know."

"I agree with you, though," I said. "And I also believe that there are some cultures represented there which existed before any sort of recorded history. They are very, very old buildings, indeed."

"There are a few legends, of course. Remarkably few, really. Most of the Kumbalari priests were killed in the 1902 earthquake and the rest of the people are pretty ignorant. After the earthquake, they stopped talking about Teku Benga altogether and most of the oral tradition had died out by the time trained scientists went up there. I suppose that's what you were after, eh? Looking for a clue. A damned dangerous expedition. Not one I'd like to risk, even by airship. Weather conditions change so quickly. The best equipped expedition could get stranded." He frowned. "It's still funny I never read about it. I thought I'd read everything on the subject. I've got our records people onto you, by the way. Trying to find out what regiment you belonged to, that sort of thing. You'll soon know who you are. Then, if you've relatives at home, we'll send you back to them."

"That's kind of you," I said.

"Least we could do. Are you an archaeologist, by the bye? Do you remember?"

"I suppose I am in a way," I admitted. "I seem to know a lot about the past and nothing at all about the —the present."

He laughed briefly. "Think I understand you. Same

56

here, really. Always digging about in the past. In many ways it was a damned sight better than today, eh?"

"I could answer that better if I could remember anything about today." I laughed in turn.

"Yes, of course." His face became serious. "You mean you know everything that happened up until the year 1902—well before you were born—and remember nothing since. It's certainly the funniest case of amnesia I've ever heard of. You must have been a pretty good scholar, if your 'memory' is that detailed. Is there anything I can do to help—trigger your memory in some way."

"You could give me a brief outline of history since 1902." I thought I had been very clever in leading into this.

He shrugged. "Nothing much has happened really. Seventy years of glorious peace, all in all. Damned dull."

"No wars at all?"

"Nothing you'd call wars, no. I suppose the last bad scrap was the Boer War."

"A war in South Africa, eh?"

"Yes—in 1910. Boers made a bid for independence. Had some justice to it, I gather. But we calmed them down, fought them for six months then made a lot of concessions. It was a pretty bloody war while it lasted, from all I've read." He took a cigarette case from his jacket pocket. "Mind if I smoke?"

"Not at all."

"Care for one?"

"Thanks." I accepted.

He grinned crookedly as he lit my cigarette with something which resembled a tinder box but which hissed—a sort of portable gas-jet, I gathered. I tried not to goggle at it as I leant forward to receive the light. "I feel like a prep-school master," he said, putting the portable gas-jet away. "Telling you all this, I mean. Still, if it helps . . ."

"It really does," I assured him. "What about the other Great Powers—France, Italy, Russia, Germany . . ."

". . . and Japan," he said, almost disapprovingly.

"What sort of trouble have they had with their colonies?"

"Not much. They deserve trouble, some of them mind you. The way the Russians and the Japanese administer their Chinese territories." He cleared his throat. "I can't say I like their methods. Still, they can be a pretty unruly lot, the Chinese." He drew deeply on his cigarette. "The Americans can be a bit soft—particularly in their Indo-Chinese colonies—but I'd rather see it that way than the other."

"The Americans have colonies?"

He laughed at this. "Seem strange, does it? Cuba, Panama, Hawaii, the Philippines, Viet Nam, Korea, Taiwan—oh, yes, they've a fair-sized Empire, all right. Not that they call it that, of course. The Greater American Commonwealth. They've had a rather strained relationship with France and Russia, but luckily England's got her fill of responsibilities. Let them get on with it, say I. Our Empire—and the Pax Britannica—will outlast them all, in my opinion."

"There were some people," I said cautiously, "in 1902 or thereabouts, who foresaw the British Empire crumbling. . . ."

Major Powell laughed heartily. "Crumbling, eh? You mean pessimists like Rudyard Kipling, Lloyd George, people like that? I'm afraid Kipling's rather been discredited these days. His heart was in the right place, of course, but it seems to me he lost faith at the last minute. If he hadn't been killed in the Boer War, he might have changed his mind, I suppose. No, I think it's fair to say that the old Empire's brought a stability to the world it has never known before. It's maintained the balance of power pretty successfully—and it hasn't done that badly for the natives, after all."

"Katmandu has certainly changed a great deal—since 1902. . . ."

He gave me another of his odd, wary looks. "Ah," he said. "You know, Bastable, if I didn't know better I could almost believe you had been on that damned mountain for seventy years. It's pretty strange, listening to a chap as young as you talking about the past in that way."

"I'm sorry," I said.

"Don't apologise. Not your fault. You'll be a joy for the brain-doctors to get their teeth into, I must say!"

I smiled. "You don't make it sound very attractive for me." I gestured towards the window. "Would you mind raising the blind?"

He tapped a little box which lay on the bedside table. The box had three switches mounted on it. "Press this one," he said. I did as he suggested and was amazed to see the blind wind itself slowly up, revealing a view of the white towers of Katmandu and, beyond them, a section of the airship park.

"They're beautiful," I said. "Those airships."

"Why, yes," he said, "I suppose they are. Take 'em a bit for granted, you know. But the airship has done a lot for India. For the Empire, come to that—for the whole world, if you like. Faster communications. Swifter trade exchanges. Greater mobility of troops."

"What surprises me," I said, "is how they can stay up. I mean, those gas-bags seem made of metal."

"Metal!" He laughed heartily. "I wish I could think you were having a joke with me, Bastable. Metal! The hulls are made of boron-fibre. It's stronger than steel and infinitely lighter. The gas is helium. There's some metal in the gondola sections, but mainly it's plastic."

" 'Plastic'—plastic what?" I asked curiously.

"Um—plastic material—it's made of chemicals— Good God, you must have heard of plastic, man. I suppose it's sort of rubber, but it can be made to harden at different strengths, in different forms, different degrees of pliability. . . ."

I gave up trying to understand Major Powell. I was never much of a scientist at the best of times. I accepted the mystery of this 'plastic' as I had accepted, while a schoolboy, the mysteries of electrical lighting. Still, it was a comfort to me, in the face of all these new wonders, that some things had not changed a great deal. Indeed, they had improved.

The carping critics of Imperialism in my own day would have been silenced pretty sharply if they had heard what I had just heard—and seen the evidence of prosperity and stability which I could now see from my window. I warmed with pride at that moment, and thanked Providence, for this vision of Utopia. Over the past seventy years the White Man had shouldered his burden jolly well, it seemed to me.

Major Powell stood up and went to the window, echoing my own thoughts as he stared out, his hands clasped over his swagger stick behind his back. "How those Victorians would have loved to see all this," he murmured. "All their ideals and dreams realised so fully. But there's still work for us to do." He turned and looked hard at me, his face half in shadow. "And a proper study of the lessons of the past, Bastable, helps us with that work."

"I'm sure you're right."

He nodded. "I know I am." He came to attention and saluted me with his swagger stick. "Well, old chap, I must be off. Duty calls."

He began to walk towards the door.

Then something happened. A dull *thump* which seemed to shake the whole building. In the distance I heard sirens sounding, bells ringing.

Major Powell's face was suddenly grim and white and his dark eyes blazed with anger.

"What is it, Major?"

"Bomb."

"Here?"

"Anarchists. Madmen. European troublemakers, almost certainly. Not the Indians at all. Germans—Russians—Jews, they've all got a vested interest in the disruption of order."

He ran from the room. Duty was indeed calling him now.

The sudden change from tranquility to violence had

taken my breath away. I lay back in the bed trying to
see what was happening outside. I saw an army motor
race across the airpark. I heard the sound of another
far-off explosion. Who on earth could be insane enough
to plot the destruction of such an Utopia as this?

## CHAPTER VI

### A Man Without a Purpose

THERE WAS LITTLE point in speculating about the
causes of the explosions any more than there was in
brooding about how I had managed to move through
Time to 1973. The events which followed the bomb in-
cidents in Katmandu moved rapidly for me as I was
shifted about the world, a bit like a rare museum speci-
men. The next morning I was bundled aboard the
'Monorail' train for Calcutta. The train was shaped
rather like an airship itself—though this was truly of
steel, all gleaming with brasswork and new paint—and
it pulled fifty carriages behind it at a terrifying speed
touching almost a hundred miles an hour on some
straight sections of its raised track. The motive power
for this incredible machine was, I learned, electricity.
Making a few short stops, we had reached Calcutta
within the day! My impression of Calcutta was of a
vast city—much larger in area than the Calcutta we
know—with gleaming towers of concrete, glass and steel
dwarfing anything I had earlier marvelled at in Katmandu. In Calcutta General Hospital I was tested by
a score of experts, all of whom pronounced themselves
baffled, and it was decided to ship me, post-haste, to
England by the first available airship. The thought of
sailing such a huge distance through the sky filled me
with some perturbation—I still could not get used to

accepting that a material lighter than steel could yet be stronger than steel and it was also difficult to conceive of Man's ability to fly six thousand miles without once landing.

The authorities preferred me in England for a number of reasons, but one of them was, of course, that they had been unable to trace a Captain Oswald Bastable as missing from any British regiment in the last decade. They had, however, checked the records of my own regiment back to 1902 and discovered, naturally, that a Captain Bastable *had* been killed at Teku Benga. I was not, now, just a puzzle for the doctors but a problem for army intelligence who were curious to know how the 'Mystery Man' (as they called me) could have assumed the identity of someone who had been dead for seventy years. I think they suspected that I might be some sort of foreign spy, but their notions were as vague as mine on that score, I later learned.

And so I took passage on the great liner of the clouds, the A.S. (for Air Ship) *Light of Dresden,* a commercial vessel owned jointly by the German firm of Krupp Luftschifahrt A.G. and the British firm of Vickers Imperial Airways. As far as registration was concerned, the *Light of Dresden* was completely British and bore the appropriate insignia on her tail-fins, but the captain was a German as were at least half the crew. The Germans, it had emerged, had been the first to develop airship flight on any sort of scale and for some time the now defunct Zeppelin Company had led the world in airship development, until Britain and America, working together, had invented the boron-fibre hull and a method of raising and lowering the ships in the air without recourse to ballast, as such. The *Light of Dresden* was equipped with this device, which involved both heating and cooling the helium gas at great speed and intensity. The massive liner also had the latest example of an electrically powered mechanical calculating machine which the people of 1973 called a 'computer' and which was capable of correcting the ship's trim automatically, without recourse to human involvement. The nature of the engine I could never quite determine. It was a single huge gas turbine engine which powered a gigantic single screw—or more properly 'propeller'—at the back of the ship. This screw was housed within the span of the great tail-fins. There were subsidiary oil-driven engines which helped adjust the ship's trim and which could swivel through 360° and which were variably pitched and reversible, able to push the ship upward or downward.

But I have not really described the most immediately impressive feature of this mighty ship of the air and that was that she was well over a thousand feet long and three hundred feet high (much of this bulk being, of course, her great gas-container). She had three decks, one beneath the other, arranged with the First Class Deck at the bottom and the Third Class Deck at the top. This single great gondola was, in fact, indivisible with the 'hull' (as the gasbag was called). At the front, in the ship's tapering nose, was the control bridge where, for all the delicate machinery 'thinking' for the ship, there were more than a dozen officers on duty at any one time.

The *Light of Dresden* needed three mooring masts to keep her safely near the ground and, when I first glimpsed her at the Calcutta Airpark (which was, in fact, about ten miles from the city), I gasped, for she made all the other ships—and there were some largish ones moored nearby—look like minnows surrounding a whale. I had already heard that she could carry 400 passengers and fifty tons of cargo without trouble. When I saw her, I believed it.

I went aboard the airship via a lift which bore me and several other passengers up through the metal cage which was the mooring mast and set us off level with a covered catwalk leading into the passage below the ship's bridge. I was travelling First Class with my 'guide', a Lt. Jagger, into whose keeping I had been put until we reached London. The amenities on the ship were astonishingly luxurious and put to shame anything to be found on the finest ocean liners of our own time. I began to relax somewhat as I looked around me. And when, later, the *Light of Dresden* let go her moorings and began to sweep with magnificent dignity into the sky, I felt almost safer than I had felt on land.

The journey from Calcutta to London took, with short stops at Karachee and Aden, 72 hours! Three days in which we had sailed over India, Africa and Europe, over three great oceans, through most kinds of weather. I had seen cities laid out before me. I had seen deserts, mountains, forests, all speeding past below. I had seen clouds which resembled organic objects. I had been *above* the clouds when it had rained, drifting tranquilly in a blue, sunny sky while the people below were drenched! I had eaten luncheon at a table as steady as a table at the Ritz (and laid with a meal almost as good as one would receive there) while we crossed the Arabian Sea and I had enjoyed my dinner while flying high above the burning sands of the Sahara Desert!

By the time we got to London, I had become quite blasé about flying. It was certainly the most comfortable form of travel I had ever experienced—and also the most civilised.

I was, I will admit, beginning to count myself the luckiest man in the history of the world. I had been taken from the grip of a deadly earthquake in 1902 and placed in the lap of luxury in 1973—a world which appeared to have solved most of its problems. Was not that the best kind—the most unbelievable kind—of good fortune? I thought so then, I must admit. I was yet to meet Korzeniowski and the others. . . .

I apologise for the digression. I must try to tell my story as it happened, give you an idea of my feelings at the time things were happening, not what I felt about everything later.

Well, at sunset of our third day, we crossed the channel and I had the experience of seeing the white cliffs of Dover far below me. Shortly after that we circled over the indescribably immense airpark at Croydon in Surrey and began our mooring manouevres. Croydon was the main airpark for London because, naturally, a big airpark can hardly be placed in the middle of Piccadilly. The Croydon Airpark was, I discovered later, the largest in the world and had a circumference of nearly twelve miles. The airpark was crowded, needless to say, with scores of airships both large and small, commercial and military, old and new. Those of us who had journeyed all the way from India had no need to pass the Customs inspection and we went through the reception buildings and took our places on the special monorail train for London. Once again I was dazed by all that was going on and was grateful for the steady, solid presence of Lieutenant Michael Jagger who steered me to my seat and took his place beside me.

Lt. Jagger had purchased a newspaper at Croydon and he offered it to me. I accepted gratefully. The size of the paper and the type were unfamiliar, as were some of the abbreviations, but I gathered the gist of most that was printed. It was the first newspaper I had seen since arriving in 1973. I had ten minutes to scan it before we reached London. In that time I learned of a new treaty which had been signed by all the Great Powers, guaranteeing a fixed scale of tariffs on many goods (how those Free Traders would have hated this!) and the recognition of various general laws, applying to all countries and their citizens It would no longer be possible in the future, the newspaper told me, for a criminal to commit a crime in Taiwan and escape across the sea to, for instance, Japanese Manchuria or even British Canada. The law, it appeared, had been agreed on unanimously by all the Great Powers, and had been inspired by the increasing incidence of lawlessness created by groups of Nihilists, Anarchists or Socialists who, the paper informed me, were bent only upon destruction for its own sake. There were other news reports, some of which I could barely understand and others of a slight nature. But I read over the reference to nihilists for it had some relation to what I had experienced on my first day in the hospital at Katmandu. As the paper suggested, these acts of violence seemed totally without logical point in a world which was steadily marching towards peace, order and justice for all. What could these madmen want? Some, of course, were native nationalists who demanded dominion status rather before they were ready for it. But the others—what did they demand? How is it possible to improve Utopia? I thought wonderingly.

And then we had arrived at Victoria Station which, in its main features, was little changed from the Victoria Station I had known in 1902.

As we disembarked from the monorail train and walked towards the exit I saw that, though it was night, the city was alive with light!

Electrical illuminations of all imaginable colours and combinations of colours blossomed from every slender tower and massive dome. Brightly lit ramps bore motor traffic around these towers on many levels, winding up and down as if supported on the very air itself.

In this London there were no ugly billboards, no illuminated advertisements, no tasteless slogans and, as we climbed into the steam-brougham and began to move along one of the ramps, I realised that there were no seedy slums of the sort found in many parts of the London I had known in 1902. Poverty had been banished! Disease had been exiled! Misery must surely be unknown!

I hope I have managed to convey some of the elation I experienced when first encountering the London of 1973. There is no question of its beauty, its cleanliness, its marvellously ordered civic amenities. There is no question that the people were well fed, cheerful, expensively dressed and, all in all, very much satisfied with their lot. During the next day or so I was taken around London by a Doctor Peters who hoped that some familiar sight might awaken my brain from its sleep. I went through with this charade because there was precious little else I could do. Eventually, I knew, they would give up. I would then be free to choose a profession—perhaps rejoin the army, since I was used to army life. But until that time I was a man without a purpose and I might just as well do what others wanted me to do. Everywhere I went I was amazed at the change which had taken place in that once dirty, fog-bound city. Fog was a thing of the past and the air was clean and sharp. Trees and shrubs and flowers grew wherever there was a space to plant them. Butterflies and birds flew about in great profusion. Fountains played in pretty squares and sometimes we would come upon a brass band entertaining the public, or a conjurer, or a Punch and Judy show, or some nigger minstrels. Not all the old buildings had gone. As fresh and clean as if they had just been built I saw Tower Bridge and the Tower of London itself, St. Paul's, the House of Parliament and Buckingham Palace (where a new King Edward—King Edward VIII, now quite an old man had his residence). The British people were, as always, accepting the best of the new and conserving the best of the old.

I began to see my visit to 1973 as a wonderful holiday. A holiday which, if I were lucky, might go on forever.

## BOOK TWO

## MORE STRANGE EVENTS—A
## REVELATION—AND SEVERAL
## DISASTERS!

## CHAPTER I

### A Question of Employment

OVER THE NEXT six months I must admit that I led a life of ease. I continued to feign amnesia and, naturally enough, nothing the doctors could do would bring back my 'memory'. Sometimes it even seemed to me that the world of 1902 had been nothing more than an extremely detailed dream. At first this worried me, but eventually it no longer came to matter to me in which period of time I 'belonged'.

I was regarded as something of a phenomenon and, for a short time, was a celebrity. Newspaper articles were written about my mysterious appearance in the Himalayan mountains and the speculation, particularly in the farthing press, grew wilder and wilder. Some of those articles were so fanciful that they even touched on the truth! I was interviewed for the kinematograph (whose coloured pictures could now talk as well as move), for the Marconiphone—now a version of the telephone which, from central stations, broadcast news reports, plays and popular music to almost every home where the receivers were amplified so that they no longer had to be lifted to the ear, but could be heard from another room if desired. I attended a reception at which the Liberal Prime Minister, Sir George Brown, was present (the Liberals had been in office for over thirty years and the Conservatives were very much a party in decline) and learned that Socialist agitation in the late 19th and eartly 20th centuries had actually had a good effect on saner political parties, like the Liberals —had, in fact, given a certain amount of impetus to many of the social improvements I had witnessed. Only recently had the serpent of Socialism—almost incredibly —begun to rear its head again in political life. Not that the creed had any support from the British people. As usual a few fanatics and neurotic intellectuals used it as a means of rationalising their own insane dreams.

During this first six months I was taken by monorail, or airship, or steamcar or electrical carriage to all parts of Britain and, of course, little was recogniseable. All major cities were modelled on similar lines to London and there was constant and rapid movement between these great 'conurbations' as they were called. Where Trade had encouraged improvements in travel and communications, these benefits had now been extended to everyone for their convenience and their pleasure.

The population had risen considerably, but the working man was as well-to-do as many middle-class people of 1902 and he had only to work a 30-hour week to keep himself in virtual luxury. And there was no problem of finding a well-appointed house to live in or a job of work to do, for the excess population of the nation was more than willing to expand beyond the British Isles. Every year thousands left to go out to all corners of the Empire: to Africa, to India, to the protectorates in China or the dominions of Australia, New Zealand and Canada. All over the world the British were settling and administering—and so civilising—even the most inaccessible areas, thanks to the invention of the airship.

At home, rural England was unspoiled and as lovely as it had ever been. No steam locomotives cast palls of smoke over trees and plants, and advertisement hoardings had long-since been abolished, as had all the uglier features of English life at the beginnings of the 20th century. Electrically-driven bicycles were available to those of the most modest income and it meant that town people could enjoy the pleasures of the countryside whenever they desired. Prices were low and wages were high (some skilled workmen getting as much as £5 per week) and if one had a few extra sovereigns to spare, then an air trip to France or Germany was often in order. By a little diligent saving, the man in the street could even afford passage by airship to visit relatives in the more distant lands of the Empire. And as for the seamier side of life, well, there was hardly any at all, for the social and moral evils which had created them had been abolished. The Suffragettes of my own day would have been happy to hear that women over thirty now had the vote and there was talk of extending the franchise to women of twenty-one. The length of girls' frocks, incidentally, was if anything shorter in London than the first I had seen in Katmandu. After some months I managed to work up courage to invite one or two pretty girls to the theatre or to a concert. Usually these were the daughters of the doctors or army officers with whom I spent my leisure time and, by our standards, the girls were rather 'forward', accepting very much an equal position in society and as outspoken as any man. After my initial surprise I found this most refreshing—as I found the plays I saw, which had many rather daring Shavian qualities (though politics, thankfully, was missing from them).

Eventually my notoriety faded and I began to feel uneasy about my long 'holiday' in the Future. I refused offers from publishers to write my memoirs (rather difficult if I really were suffering from amneisa!) and began to consider the various forms of honest employment open to me. Since my career had originally been in the army, I decided that I would prefer to continue, if possible, to serve my country in this way. However, I also entertained the notion that I should like to fly in airships and after making a few enquiries discovered that, without a great deal of training in the various functions of airship flying and navigation, I could obtain a position in the recently formed Special Air Police. There would be various exams and I should have to train for a minimum of six months, but I was confident that I could get through all that without too much trouble. It would not take me long to learn service discipline, for instance!

The new branch of the service, the Special Air Police, had been formed from the army, primarily, but there were also volunteers from the navy and the air service. It had been formed because of the need to protect civil aircraft against acts of piracy in the air, against potential saboteurs (there had been threats from fanatics but so far no serious damage done) and to protect passengers who might be bothered either by thieves aboard or criminals, for instance, on the run.

And so I applied and was accepted. I was taken to the Air Service Training School at Cardington and taught some of the mysteries of the wireless telephone —used to communicate within the ship and also with the ground, when necessary. I learned how an airship was flown and what the various technical terms meant. I was given a little practical experience in flying—this was really the only exciting part of my training—and taught the mysteries of meteorology and so forth. Although an air policeman was an army officer rather than a flyer, therefore not expected to fly a vessel, it was considered necessary to know what to do, in case of emergencies. Thus, by the end of my first year in the future (a strange sort of contradiction that, in a way) I was commissioned as a Lieutenant in His Majesty's Special Air Police and assigned to the A.S. *Loch Ness*.

For all she invited the name, the *Loch Ness* was no monster, but a trim little airship of not much more than 80 tons, with a useful lift of about 60 tons, and she handled beautifully. I was lucky to be assigned to her, though the captain pooh-poohed the necessity of having me aboard and at first was a bit cool towards me.

The bigger an airship, the more docile she normally is, but the little *Loch Ness* was quick witted, good natured and reliable. She was never a long hauler. I think the longest run we ever went on was to Gibraltar and the *Loch Ness* was not really equipped for that, being what was called a 'soft-covered' ship (her hull was fabric not 'plastic'), and she didn't have an automatic temperature control, so it was the very devil keeping her gas from expanding in the sort of heat you got in the Med. She taught me a lot about airships. It was a bit of a wrench to leave her, for you become attached to an airship rather as a navy man becomes attached to an ordinary ship. But I had only been assigned to her in order to gain some practical experience and I gather I did pretty well because the Macaphee house (who owned the *Loch Ness*) asked for my C.O. to put me on board the pride of their line, the recently built *Loch Etive*.

The *Loch Etive* was similar to the first commercial ship on which I'd flown, the *Light of Dresden*. But now that I was familiar with the details of airships, I could fully appreciate her marvels. She was a thousand feet long, with eight diesel engines mounted four a side, with reversible propellers. Her helium capacity was 12,000,000 cubic feet, contained in 24 separate bags inside the hull. Her frame was 'duralloy' and she could carry a maximum of 400 passengers and fifty tons of cargo. She could cruise easily at 100 miles an hour and her top speed was 150 mph in good weather. All her works were housed inside the hull, with the exception of the engine casings and propellers. The inspection catwalks on the top and sides of the hull were covered in and for emergencies we had parachutes, inflatable boats, life-jackets and a couple of non-rigid balloons. For the entertainment of the passengers there were kinemas, ballrooms, phonographs, deck sports and party games, restaurants—all anyone might desire concentrated in a space of a quarter of a mile floating two or three thousand feet above the surface of the Earth!

We were doing the round the world cruise on what was called the All Red Route (i.e. the colour on the map of the countries in question) but with a trip over the U.S.A. thrown in for good measure. We went from Britain via Canada and the U.S.A. down to British Ecuador and across to Australia, Hong Kong, Calcutta, Aden, Cairo and back to London. My job was to keep a look out for suspicious customers, check for weapons, bombs, that sort of thing, and—the least pleasant bit—deal with passenger complaints ranging from petty thefts and card-sharping to suspected sabotage attempts. It was a job which, on the whole, left me plenty of time to enjoy the flights and there were rarely any serious emergencies. We had an interesting selection of passengers from all nations and of all colours and creeds—Indian princes, African tribal leaders, British diplomats, American congressmen, high-ranking soldiers, and once we carried the ageing president of the Chinese Republic (which was scarcely more, I'm sorry to say, than a collection of provinces under the control of various warlords). I was particularly impressed by the education and sophistication of the native leaders, particularly the Africans, many of whom might have been mistaken for English gentlemen, save for the colour of their skins.

The man who had overall responsibility for every detail of the running of the *Loch Etive* and for every soul aboard her was old Captain Harding, who had been flying airships almost from the start, when it had been altogether a much more perilous business. He had, I learned, been one of the last to command a 'flying bomb' as they called the ships which had been filled with explosive gasses, like hydrogen, before the *Elephant* disaster of 1936, when all hydrogen-filled ships had, by international agreement, been grounded and broken up. I gathered that he was not altogether happy about commanding a passenger liner, particularly one as modern as the *Loch Etive*, but on the other hand he hated the idea of retiring. The air, he said, was his natural environment and he was damned if he was going to spend more of his life than he had to in some blasted birdcage in Balham. I got the impression that he would die if he was forced to give up flying. He was one of the most decent men I had ever met and I developed an enormous affection for him, spending much time in his company during the long periods aboard when there was nothing much to do. "They don't need a blasted captain on that gadget-run bridge," he would say, a trifle bitterly. "They could command it by telephone from London if they wanted to."

I suppose it was my strong affection for Captain Harding which led to the first disaster of my new life. A disaster which was to lead to others, of increasing consequence, until the final one. . . . But again I'm running ahead of my story.

It all began with a freakish change in the weather after we had left San Francisco, bound for British Ecuador, Tahiti, Tonga and points west. You could blame it on the elements, I suppose, or on me—but I'm rather inclined to blame an offensive little Californian 'scout-leader' called Reagan. Certainly, if Reagan had not come aboard the *Loch Etive* I should not have found myself at the centre of subsequent events—events which were to alter the destinies of a good many people and perhaps even the whole world.

## CHAPTER II

### A Man with a Big Stick

WE WERE MOORED at Berkeley Airpark, taking on cargo and passengers. Because of a delay in finding mast-space, we were a bit behind schedule and hurrying to make up the time as fast as we could. I was keeping an eye on both cargo and passengers, watching the great crates being winched into the bowels of the ship through her loading hatches underneath the lower deck. The liner was secured by about fifty thick steel cables, keeping her perfectly steady at her mast. In the bright sunlight, she cast a wide shadow across the field. I couldn't help feeling proud of her as I looked up. Her hull was silver blue and the round Union Jack shields shone on her huge tailplanes. Her particulars were emblazoned on her main hull: RMA 801 (her registration number) *Loch Etive,* London. Macaphee Lines, Edinburgh.

All about me were moored ships of American Imperial Airways, the Versailles Line, Royal Austro-Prussian Aerial Navigation Company, Imperial Russian Airship Company, Air Japan, Royal Italian Air Lines and many smaller lines, but the *Loch Etive,* it seemed to me, was the finest. She was certainly one of the most famous aerial passenger liners.

Some distance away from the airpark buildings I made out a green electric omnibus, bouncing over the turf towards our mast. These would be the last of our passengers. Rather late, I thought. I had been warned that the *William Randolph Hearst,* of American Imperial, had developed engine trouble and that, since we flew basically the same route, some of her passengers were being transferred to our ship. Probably these were they. We were almost ready to go. I watched the last item of cargo being winched aboard, saw the loading doors shut in the ship's belly, and with a sense of relief went back towards the mast.

Although there was a lift moving up and down in the central column of the mooring mast, this was for the use of passengers and officers. The ground crew were using the spiral staircase which wound round the lift shaft. I watched them hurrying up to take their positions. The fuel lighters had long-since been towed away.

At the entrance to the lift shaft I stood beside the embarkation officers who stood on both sides of the doors, checking boarding cards and tickets. There was nothing suspicious about the well-to-do Americans who were coming aboard, though they seemed a trifle annoyed at discovering they were to fly on a different ship.

I smiled a little as I saw a man at the end of the queue. He was about fifty and dressed rather ridiculously in Khaki shorts, knee stockings and green badge-festooned shirt. He carried a polished pole with a little flag on it and on his head was a wide-brimmed brown hat. His comical appearance was heightened by the look of stern self-importance on his red, lumpy face. His knees shone as redly as his nose and I wondered if he were, perhaps, a kinematograph or music hall comedian who had not had time to change. Behind him were a score of similarly clad boys of about twelve years old, with knapsacks on their backs and poles in their hands, all looking as deadly serious as the man.

"Why on earth is he dressed like that?" I asked the nearest officer.

"It's the American version of the Baden-Powell Youth Brigade," said the man. "Weren't you ever in the Brigade?"

I shook my head. "And what are these?"

"The Roosevelt Scouts," my informant told me. "The Young Roughriders, I believe they're called."

"Their leader doesn't look too young." The man had now turned his back on me, presenting a bulging posterior on which the khaki cloth threatened to burst.

"A lot of these people stay in the scouts," said the officer. "They never grow up. You know the type. Enjoy ordering the kids around."

"I'm glad I'm not in charge of that gang," I said feelingly, casting my eye over the pimply faces which glowered nervously now from beneath the brims of their hats. They had plainly not been on an airship before.

Then I noticed something which made me realise I

was forgetting my duties. Around the scout-leader's rather portly middle was strapped a leather belt and on the belt was attached a large pistol holster. When he came up to the officer inspecting tickets I waited until he was finished and then saluted politely.

"I'm sorry, sir, but I'm afraid all weapons must be given into our care until you disembark. If you wouldn't mind handing me your revolver . . ."

The man gestured angrily with his pole and tried to push past me. "Come on, boys!"

"I'm sorry, sir, I can't allow you to go aboard until . . ."

"It is my right to wear a gun if I choose. What sort of tomfool . . . ?"

"International airshipping regulations, sir. If you'll allow me to take the gun I'll get you a receipt for it and you can claim it—" I glanced at his tickets—"when you reach Sydney, Mr Reagan."

"Captain Reagan," he snapped. "Roughriders."

"Captain Reagan. Unless you give me your pistol, we can't allow you to join the flight."

"I wouldn't have this trouble on an American ship. Wait until . . ."

"International regulations apply to American ships as well as British, sir. We shall have to leave without you." I glanced significantly at my watch.

"Snotty-nosed upstart!" Purple with rage he snarled something else under his breath, then fumbled with his buckle and slid the holster off his belt. He hesitated, then handed it to me. I snapped it open and looked at the gun.

"I know," he said. "It's an air pistol. But it's very powerful."

"The regulations still apply, sir. Are—um—any more of your chaps armed in this way?"

"Of course not. I was in the Roughriders. The real Roughriders. One of the last to be disbanded. Come on, men." He pointed forward with his pole and marched into the lift, the earnest troop behind him all glaring at me in outrage at my having caused their leader to lose face. There was room in the lift for me, but I decided to use the stairs. I wasn't sure I could keep a straight face for very much longer.

Once aboard I gave the gun to the purser and received a receipt in exchange. I gave the receipt to the first steward I encountered and told him to take it to Captain Reagan's cabin. Then I went up to the bridge. We were about to let go. This was when it was worth being on the bridge and I never tired of the experience. One by one the anchor cables were released and I felt the ship surge a little as if impatient to be freed completely and get back aloft. The motors began to murmur and in the side-mirrors I could see the propellers slowly turning. The captain looked forward and then below and checked his periscopes to make sure our stern was clear. He gave the instructions and the cat-walk was drawn away from the mast, back into the hull. Now all that held the ship were the couplings attaching her to the mast.

Captain Harding spoke into the telephone. "Stand by to slip."

"Ready to slip, sir," replied the Mast Controller's voice from the receiver.

"Slip."

There was a slight jerk as the couplings fell free. The *Loch Etive* began to turn, her nose still nestling in the cone.

"All engines half-speed astern." By his tone, Captain Harding was relieved to be on his way. He stroked his white walrus moustache rather as a satisfied cat might stroke its whiskers. The diesels began to roar as we pulled out of the cone. Our bow rose.

"Half-speed ahead," said the captain. "Two degrees to port, Steering Coxswain."

"Aye, aye, sir. Two degrees to port."

"Take us up to five hundred feet, Height Coxswain, and hold steady."

"Five hundred feet, sir." The Height Cox turned

the large wheel at which he was positioned. All around us on the large bridge instruments were whirring and clicking and we were presented with a display of readings which would have thoroughly confused an old-time ship's captain.

The vast airpark fell away below us and we turned towards the sparkling ocean of San Francisco Bay. Below us we saw the hulls of the land-bound ships dwindling in size. The *Loch Etive* was behaving as beautifully as usual, almost flying herself.

Now we were over the ocean.

"Five degrees to port, Steering Coxswain," said Captain Harding, leaning over the computer console.

"Five degrees to port, sir."

We began to turn so that from our starboard portholes we could see the skyscrapers of San Francisco—painted in a thousand dazzling colours.

"Take her up to two thousand feet, Height Coxswain."

"Two thousand feet, sir."

Up we went, passing through a few wisps of cloud, into the vast sea of blue which was the sky.

"All engines full ahead."

With a great roar of power, the mighty engines pushed the ship forward. She surged on at a steady hundred and twenty miles an hour, heading for South America, carrying 385 human souls and 48 tons of cargo as effortlessly as an eagle might carry a mouse.

By that evening, the story of my encounter with the scout-leader had spread throughout the crew. Fellow officers stopped me and asked how I was getting on with 'Roughrider Ronnie' as someone had nicknamed him, but I assured them that, unless he proved to be a dangerous saboteur, I was going to avoid him punctiliously for the rest of the voyage. However, it was to emerge that he did not share my wish.

My second encounter came that night when I was making my tour of duty through the ship, normally a long and rather boring business.

The fittings of the *Loch Etive* were described in the company's brochures as 'opulent' and, particularly in the first class quarters, they were certainly lavish. Everywhere the 'plastic' was made to look exactly like marble, like oak, mahogany and teak, like steel or brass or gold. There were curtains of plush and silk drawn back from the wide observation ports running the length of the ship, there were deep carpets in blue and red and yellow, comfortable arm chairs in the lounges or on the decks. The recreation decks, restaurants, smoking rooms, bars and bathrooms were all equipped with the latest elegant gadgets and blazed with electric lighting. It was this luxury which made the *Loch Etive* one of the most expensive aerial liners in the skies, but most passengers thought it worth paying for.

By the time I had reached the third class section I was looking forward to turning in. Then, suddenly, from out of a subsidiary passage leading to the dining rooms, stormed the Captain of Roughriders himself. His face was scarlet. He was spluttering with rage and he grabbed me by the arm.

"I've a complaint!" he shouted.

I hadn't expected a compliment. I raised my eyebrows.

"About the restaurant," he continued.

"That's something to take up with the stewards, sir," I said in relief.

"I've already complained to the Chief Steward and he refused to do anything about it." He eyed me narrowly. "You are an officer, aren't you?"

I admitted it. "However, my job is to look after the security of the ship."

"What about the morals?"

I was frankly astonished. "Morals, sir?" I stuttered.

"That's what I said, young man. I have a duty to my scouts. I hardly expected them to be subjected to the indignities, the display of loose behaviour . . . Come with me."

Out of curiosity more than anything else, I allowed

him to lead me into the dining room. Here a rather insipid jazz band was playing and a few couples were dancing. At the tables people were eating or talking and not a few were staring at the table where all twenty boy Roughriders were seated.

"There!" hissed Reagan. "There! What do you say now?"

"I can't see anything, sir."

"Nobody told me that I was coming aboard a flying Temple of Jezebel! Immoral women displaying themselves—look! Look!" I was bound to say that the girls were wearing rather scanty evening frocks, but nothing one would not see every night in London. "And disgusting music—jungle music!" He pointed at the bored-looking band on the rostrum. "And, worse than that," (he drew closer and hissed in my ear) "there are, young man, *niggers* eating right next to us. What kind of a decent ship do you call this?"

At the nearest table to the scouts sat a party of Indian civil servants who had recently finished their exams in London and were on their way to Hong King. They were well-dressed and sat quietly talking among themselves.

"White boys being forced to eat elbow to elbow with niggers," Reagan continued. "We were transferred without our agreement to this ship, you know. On a decent American ship . . ."

The Chief Steward came up. He gave me a weary, apologetic look. I thought of a solution.

"Perhaps this passenger and his boys could eat in their cabins," I suggested to the steward.

"That won't do!" There was a hard, mad gleam in Reagan's eye. "I have to supervise them. Make sure they eat properly and keep themselves clean."

I was ready to give up when the steward suggested, poker-faced, that screens might be placed around the table. They would not keep out the music, of course, but at least the captain and his lads would not be forced to see either the scantily dressed ladies or the

Indian civil servants. Reagan accepted this compromise with poor grace and was about to return to his table when one of the boys came rushing up, his handkerchief over his mouth, his face very green indeed. Another boy followed. "I think Dubrowski's being airsick, sir."

I hurried off, leaving Reagan shouting wildly for a 'medic'.

For all that it is primarily a psychological illness, airsickness can be catching and I soon learned to my relief that Reagan and his entire troop had gone down with it. When, two days later, we reached Quito in British Ecuador, I had heard nothing more of the scoutmaster, though I believe one of the ship's doctors had been kept pretty busy.

We made a quick stopover at Quito and took on a few passengers, some airmail and a couple of cages of live monkeys bound for a zoo in Australia.

By the time we headed out over the Pacific, Reagan was well known to crew and passengers alike and though there were some who supported him, he had become to most a figure of some considerable entertainment value.

Captain Harding had not directly encountered Reagan and he was faintly amused by the reports he had heard concerning my own embarrassment. "You must be more firm with him, Lieutenant Bastable. It is a particular knack, you know, controlling a difficult passenger."

"This one's mad, skipper." We were having a drink in the little bar above the control cabin which was especially for the officers. "You ought to see his eyes," I said.

Harding smiled sympathetically, but it was obvious he put much of my trouble down to my own inexperience and the fact that I was essentially a groundman.

Our crossing of that wide stretch of ocean between

South America and the first of the South Sea islands was as peaceful as usual and we flew through blue and sunny skies.

By the time we sighted Puka Puka, however, we were receiving telephoned messages about a freak storm blowing up in the Papeete region. Heavy electrical interference soon cut these messages off, but at this stage we had no trouble keeping the ship in trim. Stewards warned the passengers that it was likely to get a bit bumpy as we neared Tahiti, but we expected to reach the island on time. We took the ship up to 2,500 feet and hoped to avoid the worst of the winds. The engineers working in the diesel nacelles were ordered to keep the *Loch Etive* at full speed ahead when we hit the disturbance.

A few minutes later it became strangely dark and a peculiar, cold grey light streamed through our portholes. The electrics were switched on.

Next moment we had plunged into the storm and heard the thunder of hailstones beating against the huge hull. The sound was like a thousand machine guns going off at once and we could hardly hear each other speak. The temperature dropped dramatically and we shivered with cold until the ship's heating system responded to our need. As thunder and lightning crashed and flashed around us the *Loch Etive* shook a little but her engines roared defiantly back and we plunged on into the swirling black cloud. There was no danger of lightning striking our fully insulated hull. Occasionally the clouds would part to show us the sea boiling about below.

"Glad I'm not down there," said Captain Harding with a grin. "Makes you glad the airship was invented."

Soft music began to sound from the telephone receivers on the bridge. The skipper told his second officer to switch it off. "Never could understand the theory behind that."

My stomach turned over as the ship fell a few feet and then recovered. I began to feel little tendrils of fear creep into my mind. It was the first time I had felt nervous aboard an airship since Major Powell had picked me up at Teku Benga. That seemed centuries ago now.

"Very dirty weather, indeed," murmured the captain. "Worst I've ever known at this time of year." He buttoned up his jacket. "How's our height, Height Cox?"

"Holding steady, sir."

The door to the bridge opened and the third officer came in. He was furious.

"What's up?" I said.

"Damn it!" he swore. "I've just had a tangle with your chap, Bastable. Bloody fellow Reagan! Screaming about life-rafts and parachutes. He's berserk. Never known a passenger like it. Says we're going down. I've had the most awful shouting match with him. He wanted to see you, sir." The third officer addressed the captain.

I smiled at Harding who grinned wryly back. "What did you tell him, number three?"

"I think I calmed him down in the end, sir." The third officer frowned. "It was all I could do to stop myself punching him on the jaw."

"Better not do that, number three." The captain took out his pipe and began to light it. "Not very good for the company if he sues us, eh? And we've a special responsibility, too—courtesy to American Imperial, that sort of thing."

The third officer turned to me. "I suppose he's told you he's got powerful political connections in America. That he'll have you drummed out of the service."

I laughed. "No, I haven't had that one yet."

Then the hail hit us even harder and the wind howled in fury as if at our insolence in remaining airborne. The ship dropped horribly and then re-adjusted. She shuddered the length of her hull. It was black as night outside. Lightning spat at us on all sides. With some idea of reassuring the passengers and, since there was nothing practical I could do on the bridge, I went towards the door.

And at that moment it burst open and in rushed Reagan, the picture of terrified anger, his white-faced scouts behind him.

Reagan gesticulated wildly with his pole as he advanced towards Captain Harding. "I've a duty to these boys. Their parents entrusted me with their lives! I demand that life-rafts and parachutes be issued to us at once!"

"Please return to your cabin, sir," said Harding firmly. "The ship is perfectly safe. It is much better, however, if passengers are not wandering about—particularly on the bridge. If you are nervous, one of the ship's doctors will give you a sedative."

Reagan screamed something incoherent in reply. Captain Harding put his pipe in his mouth and turned his back.

"Please leave my bridge, sir."

I stepped forward. "I think you'd better—"

But Reagan had put his beefy hand on Captain Harding's shoulder. "Now just look here, captain. I've a right . . ."

The skipper turned, speaking very coldly. "I wonder if one of you gentlemen would mind escorting this passenger back to his cabin?"

The third officer and I took hold of Reagan and dragged him back. He made surprisingly little resistance. He was trembling all over. We took him out of the bridge and into the passage where I called for a couple of ratings to take over from me, for I was furious at the way Reagan had treated Harding and did not trust myself to deal calmly with the man.

When I got back to the bridge Harding was sucking on his pipe as if nothing had happened. "Damned hysterical woman," he said to no one in particular. "Hope this storm blows over soon."

## CHAPTER III

### Disaster—and Disgrace!

WHEN AT LAST we reached Tahiti and began to drop through the clouds in the hope of mooring, it became evident that a full-scale typhoon had hit the island. The ship shuddered and swerved about in the sky and it was all we could do to keep her in reasonable trim.

Below, whole groves of palms had been bent to the ground by the wind and a number of buildings had been severely damaged. Only the three mooring masts in the airpark stood upright and to these there were already two ships anchored. A whole web of extra cables had been used to secure them.

After sizing up the situation the skipper ordered the Steering Cox to keep circling over the airpark and then left the bridge. "Back in a moment," he said.

The third officer winked at me. "Gone for a shot of rum, I shouldn't wonder. Can't blame him, what with the storm *and* that Reagan chap."

The big ship continued to circle at full speed against the howling force of a storm which showed no sign of abating. Every so often I looked down at the airpark and saw that the savage winds still swept it.

A quarter of an hour passed and still the captain did not reappear on the bridge. "It's not like him to be gone so long," I said.

The third officer tried to get through to the captain's cabin by telephone but there was no reply. "Expect he's on his way back," he said.

Another five minutes passed and then the third officer told a rating to go and look in the captain's cabin to make sure he was all right.

A couple of moments later the rating came running back, a look of terrible consternation on his face. "It's the captain, sir. Up in the parachute lockers—hurt, sir. There's a doctor coming."

"Parachute lockers? What's he doing up there?" Since it was impossible for any of the other airship officers to leave the bridge, I followed the rating down the narrow passage and up the short companion ladder leading to the officers' quarters. We passed the captain's cabin and reached another short ladder to the catwalk between the lockers where the lifesaving equipment was stored. The light was dim here, but I could make out the captain lying at the foot of the ladder, his face twisted in pain. I knelt beside him.

"Fell down the damned ladder." The captain spoke with difficulty. "Broken my leg, I think." The ship shook as another great gust of wind hit her. "Blasted Reagan feller—found him trying to open the parachute lockers. Went up to make him come down. He pushed me—ah!"

"Where's Reagan now, sir?"

"Ran off. Scared, I suppose."

The doctor arrived and inspected the leg. "A fracture, I'm afraid. You'll be grounded for quite a while, captain."

I saw the look in the captain's eyes when he heard the doctor's words. It was a look of pure fear. If he was grounded now it would mean he was grounded forever. He was already well past retirement age. Scoutleader Reagan had successfully ended Harding's flying days—and therefore ended his life. If I had been close to Reagan at that moment, I think I would have killed him!

Eventually the storm blew itself out and within half-an-hour we were manoeuvring into the waiting cone on the airpark mast. The sky was completely clear and the sun was shining and Tahiti looked as beautiful as ever. Apart from a bit of damage to some buildings and a few broken trees, you might never have known that the typhoon had been there.

Later, I watched the medical orderlies pick up the captain's stretcher and carry it down to the nose. I saw the lift bear Captain Harding down to the ground to where the ambulance awaited.

I was miserable. And I was sure I would never see the skipper again. God, how I hated Reagan for what he had done! I have never hated anyone so much in my life. Harding had been one of the few people in this world of the future to whom I could properly relate—perhaps because Harding was an old man and therefore more of my world than of his own—and now he was gone. I felt damned lonely, I can tell you. I decided to keep a special watch on 'Captain' Reagan now.

Tonga came and went and we were soon heading for Sydney, making a speed of just under 120 mph against a head wind which was scarcely more than a gentle breeze compared with the typhoon we had recently experienced.

For the whole time since arriving in Tahiti, Reagan and his scouts only left their cabins to eat their meals behind their foolish screens.

At least he seemed cowed by his own stupidity and he knew he had got off lightly regarding the affair of the parachute lockers. When, once, we met in a corridor, he lowered his eyes and did not speak to me as we passed each other.

But then came the incident which was to lead to the real disasters of the coming months.

On the last night before we were due to reach Sydney, a call came through to the bridge from the third class dining room. Trouble of some kind. It was my duty to go there and sort it out.

Reluctantly, I left the bridge and made my way to the dining hall. In the corner near the galley door there was confusion. White-coated stewards, ratings in midnight blue, men in evening dress and girls in short frocks, were all scuffling about, dragging at a man dressed in the all-too-familiar khaki shorts and green shirt of a Young Roughrider. Around the edges of this melee stood a number of frightened boy scouts. I glimpsed Reagan's face then. He was clutching his pole in his hands and striking out at those who tried to hold him. His eyes were staring, his face was purple and he resembled some ludicrous tableau of Custer at the Victory of Little Big Horn. He was screaming incoherently and I caught only a single, distasteful word:

"Niggers! Niggers! Niggers!"

To one side, some of the Indian civil servants were talking to the young officer who had summoned me.

"What's all this about, Muir?" I asked.

Muir shook his head. "As far as I can tell this gentleman," (he indicated the civil servant) "asked if he could borrow the salt from Mr Reagan's table. Mr Reagan hit him, sir, then started on this gentleman's friends . . ."

I saw now that there was a livid mark on the Indian's forehead.

I pulled myself together as best I could and called out: "All right, everybody. Let him go. Could you please stand back? Stand back, please."

Gratefully, the passengers and crew members moved away from Reagan who stood panting and glaring and plainly out of his mind. With a sudden movement he leapt onto a nearby table, hunched with his stick at the ready.

I tried to speak civilly, remembering that it was my duty to protect both the good name of the shipping company, to protect the name of my own service and to give Mr Reagan no opportunity to sue anyone or use his political connections to harm anyone. It was hard to remember all this, particularly when I hated the man so much. I did my best to feel sorry for him, to humour him. "It's over now, Captain Reagan. If you will apologise to the gentleman you struck—"

"Apologise? To that scum!" With a snarl, Regan aimed a blow at me with his pole. I grabbed it and dragged him off the table. If I had struck him then, in order to calm him down, I might have been forgiven. But it was as if his own madness was infectious.

Reagan put his snarling face up against mine and growled: "Give me my stick, you damned nigger-loving British sissy!"

It was too much for me.

I don't actually remember striking the first blow. I remember punching and punching and being pulled back. I remember seeing his blood flowing from his cut face. I remember shrieking something about what he had done to the skipper. I remember his pole clutched in my hands rising and falling and then I was being pulled back by several ratings and everything became suddenly, terrifyingly calm and Reagan lay on the floor, bruised and bloody and completely insensible, perhaps dead.

I turned, dazed, and saw the shocked faces of the scouts, the passengers, the crew.

I saw the second officer, now in command, come running up. I saw him look down at Reagan's body and say "Is he dead?"

"He should be," said someone. "But he isn't."

The second officer came up to me and there was pity in his face. "You poor devil, Bastable," he said. "You shouldn't have done it, old man. You're in trouble now, I'm afraid."

Of course I was suspended from duty as soon as I got to Sydney and reported to the local S.A.P. headquarters. Nobody was unsympathetic, especially when they had heard the full story from the other officers of the *Loch Etive*. But Reagan had already given *his* story to the evening papers. The worst was happening. AMERICAN TOURIST ATTACKED BY POLICE OFFICER, said the *Sydney Herald*, and most of the reports were of the most sensational kind and most of them were on the front page. The company and the name of the ship were mentioned; His Majesty's most recently formed service, the Special Air Police, were mentioned ('Is this what we may expect from those commissioned to protect us?' asked one paper). Passengers had been interviewed and a non-committal statement from the company's Sydney office was quoted. I had said nothing to the press, of course, and some of the newspapers had taken this as an admission that I had set upon Reagan without provocation and tried to kill him. Then I received a cable from my C.O. in London. RETURN AT ONCE.

Depression filled my mind and set there, hard and cold, and I could think nothing but black thoughts on the journey back to London in the aerial man-o'-war *Relentless*. There was no possible excuse, as far as the army was concerned, for my behaviour. I knew I would be court-martialed and almost certainly cashiered. It was not a pleasant prospect.

When I arrived in London I was taken immediately to the S.A.P. headquarters near the small military airpark at Limehouse. I was confined to barracks, pending a decision from my C.O. and the War Office as to what to do with me.

As it emerged, Reagan was persuaded to drop his charges against everyone and was further persuaded to admit that he had seriously provoked me, but I had still behaved badly and a court-martial was still in order.

Several days after hearing about Reagan's decision, I was summoned to the C.O.'s office and asked to sit down. Major-General Fry was a decent type and very much of the old school. He understood what had happened but put his position bluntly:

"Look here, Bastable, I know what you've been through. First the amnesia and now this—well, this fit of yours, if you like. Fit of rage, what? I know. But you see we can't be sure you won't have another. I mean— well, the old brain-box and all that—a trifle shaky, um?"

I smiled wryly at him, I remember. "You think I'm mad, sir?"

"No, no, no, of course not. Nervy, say. Anyway, the long and short of it is this, Bastable: I want your resignation."

He coughed with embarrassment and offered me a cigar without looking at me. I refused.

Then I stood up and saluted. "I understand perfectly, sir, and I appreciate why you want to do it this way. It's decent of you, sir. Of course you shall have my resignation from the service. Morning all right, sir?"

"Fine. Take your time. Sorry to lose you. Good luck, Bastable. I gather you needn't worry about Macaphees taking any action. Captain Harding spoke up for you with the owners. So did the rest of the officers, I gather."

"Thank you for letting me know, sir."

"Not at all. Cheerio, Bastable." He got up and shook my hand. "Oh, by the way, your brother wants to see you. I got a message. He'll meet you at the Royal Aeronautical Club this evening."

"My brother, sir?"

"Didn't you know you had one?"

I did have a brother. In fact I had three. But I had left them behind in 1902.

Feeling as if I had gone completely mad I left the C.O.'s office, went back to my quarters, composed my letter of resignation, packed my few things into a bag, changed into civilian clothes and took an electric hansom to Piccadilly and the Royal Aeronautical Club.

Why should someone claim to be my brother? There was probably a simple explanation. A mistake, of course, but I could not be sure.

## CHAPTER IV

### A Bohemian 'Brother'

AS I SAT back in the smoothly moving cab, I stared out of the windows and tried to collect my thoughts. Since the incident with Reagan I had been stunned and only now that I had left my barracks behind me was I beginning to realise the implications of my action. I also realised that I had got off rather lightly, all things considered. Yet my efforts to become accepted by the society of 1974 had, it now appeared, been completely wasted. I was much more of an outsider than when I had first arrived. I had disgraced my uniform and put myself beyond the pale.

What was more, the euphoric dream had begun to turn into a crazy nightmare. I took out my watch. It was only three o'clock in the afternoon. Not evening by anyone's standards. I was uncertain as to what kind of reception I might have at the R.A.C. I was, of course, a member, but it was quite possible they would wish me to resign, as I had resigned from the S.A.P. I couldn't blame anyone for wishing this. After all, I was likely to embarrass the other members. I would leave my visit until the last possible moment. I tapped on the roof and told the cabbie to stop at the nearest pedestrian ingress, then I got out of the cab, paid my fare and began to wander listlessly around the arcades beneath the graceful columns supporting the traffic levels. I stared at the profusion of exotic goods displayed in the shop windows; goods brought from all corners of the Empire, reminding me of places I might never see again. Searching for escape I went into a kinema and watched a musical comedy set in the 16th century and featuring an American actor called Humphrey Bogart playing Sir Francis Drake and a Swedish actress (Bogart's wife, I believe) called Greta Garbo as Queen Elizabeth. Oddly, it is one of the clearest impressions I have of that day.

At about seven o'clock I turned up at the club and slipped unnoticed into the pleasant gloom of the bar, decorated with dozens of airship mementoes. There were a few chaps chatting at tables but luckily nobody recognised me. I ordered a whisky and soda and drank it down rather quickly. I had had several more by the time someone touched me on the arm and I turned suddenly, fully expecting to be asked to leave.

Instead I was confronted by the cheerful grin on the face of a young man dressed in what I had learned was the fashion amongst the wilder undergraduates at Oxford. His black hair was worn rather long and brushed back without a parting. He wore what was virtually a frock coat, with velvet lapels, a crimson cravat, a brocade waistcoat and trousers cut tightly to the knee and then allowed to flare at the bottoms. We should have recognised it in 1902 as being very similar to the dress affected by the so-called aesthetes. It was deliberately Bohemian and dandified and I regarded people who wore this 'uniform' with some suspicion. They were not my sort at all. Where I had escaped notice, this young man had the disapproving gaze of all. I was acutely embarrassed.

He seemed unaware of the reaction he had created in the club. He took my limp hand and shook it warmly. "You're brother Oswald, aren't you?"

"I'm Oswald Bastable," I agreed. "But I don't think I'm the one you want. I have no brother."

He put his hand on one side and smiled. "How d'you know, eh? I mean, you're suffering from amnesia, aren't you?"

"Well, yes. . . ." It was perfectly true that I could hardly claim to have lost my memory and then deny that I had a brother. I had placed myself in an ironic situation. "Why didn't you come forward earlier?" I countered. "When there was all that stuff about me in the newspapers?"

He rubbed his jaw and eyed me sardonically. "I was abroad at the time," he said. "In China, actually. Bit cut off there."

"Look here," I said impatiently, "you know damn' well you're not my brother. I don't know what you want, but I'd rather you left me alone."

He grinned again. "You're quite right. I'm not your brother. The name's Dempsey actually—Cornelius Dempsey. I thought I'd say I was your brother in order to pique your curiosity and make sure you met me. Still," (he gave me that sardonic look again) "it's funny you should be suffering from total amnesia and yet know that you haven't got a brother. Do you want to stay and chat here or go and have a drink somewhere else?"

"I'm not sure I want to do either, Mr Dempsey. After all, you haven't explained why you chose to deceive me in this way. It would have been a cruel trick, if I had believed you."

"I suppose so," he said casually. "On the other hand you might have a good reason for *claiming* amnesia. Maybe you've something to hide? Is that why you didn't reveal your real identity to the authorities?"

"What I have to hide is my own affair. And I can assure you, Mr Dempsey, that Oswald Bastable is the only name I have ever owned. Now—I'd be grateful if you would leave me alone. I have plenty of other problems to consider."

"But that's why I'm here, Bastable, old chap. To help you solve those problems. I'm sorry if I've offended you. I really did come to help. Give me half-an-hour." He glanced around him. "There's a place round the corner where we can have a drink."

I sighed. "Very well." I had nothing to lose, after all. I wondered for a moment if this dandified young man, so cool and self-possessed, actually knew what had really happened to me. But I dismissed the idea.

We left the R.A.C. and turned into the Burlington

Arcade, which was one of the few places which had not changed much since 1902, and stepped into Jermyn Street. At last Cornelius Dempsey stopped at a plain door and rapped several times with the brass knocker until someone answered. An old woman peered out at us, recognised Dempsey, and admitted us to a dark hallway. From somewhere below came the sound of voices and laughter and, by the smell, I judged the place to be a drinking club of some kind. We went down some stairs and entered a poorly lit room in which were set out a number of plain tables. At the tables sat young men and women dressed in the same Bohemian fashion as Dempsey. One or two of them greeted him as we made our way among the tables and sat down in a niche. A waiter came up at once and Dempsey ordered a bottle of red Vin Ordinaire. I felt extremely uncomfortable, but not as badly as I had felt at my own club. This was my first glimpse of a side of London life I had hardly realised existed. When the wine came I drank down a large glass. If I were to be an outcast, I thought bitterly, then I had best get used to this kind of place.

Dempsey watched me drink, a look of secret amusement on his face. "Never been to a cellar club before, eh?"

"No." I poured myself another drink from the bottle.

"You can relax here. The atmosphere's pretty free and easy. Wine all right?"

"Fine." I sat back in my chair and tried to appear confident. "Now what's all this about, Mr Dempsey?"

"You're out of work at the moment, I take it?"

"That's an understatement. I'm probably unemployable."

"Well, that's just it. I happen to know there's a job going if you want one. On an airship. I've already talked to the master and he's willing to take you on. He knows your story."

I became suspicious. "What sort of a job, Mr. Dempsey? No decent skipper would . . ."

"This skipper is one of the most decent men ever to command a ship." He dropped his bantering manner and spoke seriously. "I admire him tremendously and I know you'd like him. He's straight as a die."

"Then why—?"

"His ship is a bit of a crate. Not one of your big liners or anything like that. It's old-fashioned and slow and carries cargo mainly. Cargo that other people aren't interested in. Small jobs. Sometimes dangerous jobs. You know the kind of ship."

"I've seen them." I sipped my wine. The chance was the only sort I might expect and I was incredibly lucky to get it. It was logical that small 'tramp' airships would be short of trained airshipmen when the rewards for working for the big ships were so much greater. And yet, at that moment, I hardly cared. I was still full of bitterness at my own foolishness. "But are you sure the captain knows the whole story? I was chucked out of the army for good reason, you know."

"I know the reason," said Dempsey earnestly. "And I approve of it."

"Approve? Why?"

"Just say I don't like Reagan's type. And I admire what you did for those Indians he attacked. It proves you're a decent type with your heart in the right place."

I'm not sure I appreciated such praise from that young man. I shrugged. "Defending the Indians was only incidental," I told him. "I hated Reagan, because of what he did to my skipper."

Dempsey smiled. "Put it how you like, Bastable. Anyway, the job's going. Want it?"

I finished my second glass of wine and frowned. "I'm not sure. . . ."

Dempsey poured me another glass. "I'm not trying to persuade you to do something you don't want to—but I might point out that few people will want to employ you as anything more than a deckhand—for a while, at least."

"I'm aware of that."

Dempsey lit a long cheroot. "Perhaps you have friends who've offered you a ground job?"

"Friends? No. I've no friends." It was true. Captain Harding had been the nearest thing I had had to a friend.

"And you've experience of airships. You could handle one if you had to?"

"I suppose so. I passed an exam equivalent to a Second Officer's. I'm probably a bit weak on the practical side."

"You'll soon learn that, though."

"How do you happen to know the captain of an air freighter?" I asked. "Aren't you a student?"

Dempsey lowered his eyes. "You mean an undergraduate? Well, I was. But that's another story altogether. I've followed your career, you know, since you were found on that mountain top. You captured my imagination, you might say."

I laughed then, without much humour. "Well, I suppose it's generous of you to try to help me. When can I see this captain of yours?"

"Tonight?" Dempsey grinned eagerly. "We could go down to Croydon in my car. What do you say?"

I shrugged. "Why not?"

# CHAPTER V

## Captain Korzeniowski

DEMPSEY DROVE DOWN to Croydon at some speed but I was forced to admire the way he controlled the old-fashioned Morgan steamer. We reached Croydon in half-an-hour.

The town of Croydon is an airpark town. It owes its existence to the airpark and everywhere you look there are reminders of the fact. Many of the hotels are named after famous airships and the streets are crowded with flyers of every nationality. It is a brash, noisy town compared with most and must be quite similar to some of the old seaports of my own age (perhaps I should use the future tense for all this and say 'will be' and so on, but I find it hard to do, for all these events took place, of course, in my personal past).

Dempsey drove us into the forecourt of a small hotel in one of the Croydon backstreets. The hotel was called *The Airman's Rest* and had evidently been a coaching inn in earlier days. It was, needless to say, in the old part of the town and contrasted rather markedly with the bright stone and glass towers which dominated most of Croydon.

Dempsey took me through the main parlour full of flyers of the senior generation who plainly preferred the atmosphere of *The Airman's Rest* to that of the more salubrious hotels. We went up a flight of wooden stairs and along a passage until we came to a door at the end. Dempsey knocked.

"Captain? Are you receiving visitors, sir?"

I was surprised at the genuine tone of respect with which the young man addressed the unseen captain.

"Enter." The voice was harsh and guttural. A foreign voice.

We walked into a comfortable bed-sitting room. A fire blazed in the grate, providing the only illumination. In a deep leather armchair sat a man of about sixty. He had an iron grey beard cut in the Imperial style and hair to match. His eyes were blue-grey and their gaze was steady, penetrating, totally trustworthy. He had a great beak of a nose and a strong mouth. When he stood up he was relatively short but powerfully built. His handshake was dry and firm as Dempsey introduced us.

"Captain Korzeniowski, this is Lieutenant Bastable."

"How do you do, lieutenant." The accent was thick but the words were clear. "Delighted to meet you."

"How do you do, sir. I think you'd better refer to me as plain 'mister'. I resigned from the S.A.P. today. I'm a civilian now."

Korzeniowski smiled and turned towards a heavy oak sideboard. "Would you care for a drink—*Mister* Bastable?"

"Thank you, sir. A whisky?"

"Good. And you, young Dempsey?"

"A glass of that Chablis I see, if you please, captain."

"Good."

Korzeniowski was dressed in a heavy white roll-neck pullover. His trousers were the midnight blue of a civil flying officer. Over a chair near the desk, against the far wall, I saw his jacket with its captain's rings, and on top of that his rather battered cap.

"I put the proposal to Mr Bastable, sir," said Dempsey as he accepted his glass. "And that's why we're here."

Korzeniowski fingered his lips and looked thoughtfully at me. "Doubtless," he murmured. "Doubtless." After giving us our drinks he went back to the sideboard and poured himself a modest whisky, filling the glass up with soda. "You know I need a second officer pretty badly. I could do with a man with rather more experience of flying, but I can't get anyone in England and I don't want the type of man I'd be likely to find out of England. I've read about you. You're hot-tempered, eh?"

I shook my head. Suddenly it seemed to me that I wanted very much to serve with Captain Korzeniowski for I had taken an instant liking to the man. "Not normally, sir. These were—well, special circumstances, sir."

"That's what I gathered. I had a fine second officer until recently. Chap named Marlowe. Got into some trouble in Macao." The captain frowned and took a cheroot case from his desk. He offered me one of the hard, black sticks of tobacco and I accepted. Dempsey refused with a grin. As he spoke, Captain Korzeniowski kept his eyes on me and I felt he was reading my soul. He spoke rather ponderously and all his actions were slow, calculated. "You were found in the Himalayas. Lost your memory. Trained for the air police. Got into a fight with a passenger on the *Loch Etive*. Lost your temper. Hurt him badly. Passenger was a boor, eh?"

"Yes, sir." The cheroot was surprisingly mild and sweet-smelling.

"Objected to eating with some Indians, I gather?"

"Among other things, sir."

"Good." Korzeniowski gave me another of his sharp penetrating glances.

"Reagan was responsible, sir, for our skipper's breaking his leg. It meant that the old man would be grounded for good. The skipper couldn't bear that idea, sir."

Korzeniowski nodded. "Know how he feels. Captain Harding. Used to know him. Fine airshipman. So your crime was an excess of loyalty, mm? That *can* be a pretty serious crime in some circumstances, eh?"

His words seemed to have an extra significance I couldn't quite divine. "I suppose so, sir."

"Good."

Dempsey said, "I think, sir, that temperamentally at any rate he's one of us."

Korzeniowski raised his hand to silence the young man. The captain was staring into the fire, deep in consideration of something. A few moments later he turned round and said, "I am a Pole, Mr Bastable. A naturalised Briton, but a Pole by birth. If I went back to my homeland, I would be shot. Do you know why?"

"No, sir."

The captain smiled and spread his hands. "Because I am a Pole. That is why."

"You are an exile, sir? The Russians . . . ?"

"Exactly. The Russians. Poland is part of their empire. I felt that this was wrong, that nations should be free to decide their own destinies. I said so—many years ago. I was heard to say so. And I was exiled.

That was when I joined the British Merchant Air Service. Because I was a Polish patriot." He shrugged. I wondered why he was telling me this, but I felt there must be a point to it, so I listened respectfully. Finally he looked up at me. "So you see, Mr. Bastable, we are both outcasts, in our way. Not because we wish it, but because we have no choice."

"I see, sir." I was still puzzled, but said no more.

"I own my own ship," said Korzeniowski. "She isn't much to look at, but she's a good little craft. Will you join her, Mr Bastable?"

"I would like to, sir. I'm very grateful . . ."

"You've no need to be grateful, Mr Bastable. I need a second officer and you need a position. The pay isn't very high. Five pounds a month, all found."

"Thank you, sir."

"Good."

I still wondered what connection there could possibly be between the young Bohemian and the old airship skipper. They seemed to know each other quite well.

"I think you'll be able to find accommodation for the night in this hotel, if it suits you," Captain Korzeniowski continued. "Join the ship tomorrow. Eight o'clock be all right?"

"Fine, sir."

"Good."

I picked up my bag and looked expectantly at Dempsey. The young man glanced at the captain, grinned at me and patted me on the arm. "Get yourself settled in here. I'll join you later. One or two things to discuss with the captain."

Still in something of a daze I said goodbye to my new skipper and left the room. As I closed the door I heard Dempsey say, "Now, about the passengers, sir . . ."

Next morning I took an omnibus to the airpark.

There were dozens of airships moored there, coming and going like monstrous bees around a monstrous hive. In the autumn sunshine the hulls of the vessels shone like silver or gold or alabaster. Before he had left the previous night Dempsey had given me the name of the ship I was to join. She was called *The Rover* (a rather romantic name, I thought) and the airpark authorities had told me she was moored to Number 14 mast. I was, in the cold light of day as it were, beginning to wonder if I had not acted rather hastily in accepting the position, but it was too late for second thoughts. I could always leave the ship later if I found that I wasn't up to what was expected of me.

When I got to Number 14 mast I found that she had been shifted to make room for a big Russian freighter with a combustible cargo which had to be taken off in a hurry. Nobody seemed to know where *The Rover* was now moored.

Eventually, after half-an-hour of fruitless wandering about, I was told to go to Number 38 mast, right on the other side of the park. I trudged beneath the huge hulls of liners and cargo ships, dodging between the shivering mooring cables, circumnavigating the steel girders of the masts, until at last I saw Number 38 and my new craft.

She was battered and she needed painting, but she was as brightly clean as the finest liner. She had a hard hull, obviously converted from a soft, fabric cover of the old type. She was swaying a little at her mast and seemed, by the way she moved in her cables, very heavily loaded. Her four big, old-fashioned engines were housed in outside nacelles which had to be reached by means of partly-covered catwalks, and her inspection walks were completely open to the elements. I felt like someone who had been transferred from the *Oceanic* to take up a position on a tramp steamer. For all that I came from a period of time before any airship had seemed a practical means of travel, my interest in *The Rover* was almost one of historical curiosity as I looked her over. She was certainly weather-beaten. The silvering on her hull was beginning to flake and the lettering of her number (806), name and registration (London) had peeled off in places. Since it was illegal to have even a partially obliterated registration, there were a couple of airshipmen hanging in a pulley platform suspended from the topside catwalk, touching up the transfers with black creosote. She was even older than my first ship, the *Loch Ness,* and much more primitive, with a slightly piratical look about her. I doubted she boasted such things as computers, temperature regulators or anything but the most unsophisticated form of wireless telephone, and her speed could not have been much over 80 mph.

I had a moment of trepidation as I stood there, watching her turn sluggishly in her cables and then, reluctantly, swing back to her original position. She was about 600 feet long and not an inch of her looked as if it should have been passed as airworthy. I began to climb the mast, hoping that my lateness had not held the ship up.

I got to the top of the mast and entered the cone. From cone to ship there was a narrow gangplank with rope sides. It bent as I set foot on it and began to cross. No special covered gangways for *The Rover,* no reinforced plastic walls so that passengers needn't see the ground a hundred feet below. A peculiar feeling of satisfaction began to creep over me. After my initial shock, I was beginning to like the idea of flying in this battered old tramp of the skylanes. She had a certain style about her and there was nothing fancy about her fixtures. She had something of the aura of the early pioneer ships which Captain Harding had often reminisced about.

As I reached the circular embarkation platform I was greeted by an airshipman in a dirty pullover. He jerked his thumb towards a short aluminium companionway which wound up from the centre of the platform. "You the new number two, sir? Captain's expecting you on the bridge."

I thanked him and climbed the steps to emerge on

the bridge. It was deserted but for the short, stocky man in the well-pressed but threadbare uniform of a Merchant Air Service captain. He turned, his blue-grey eyes as steady and as contemplative as ever, one of his black cheroots in his mouth, his grey Imperial jutting forward as he stepped towards me and shook my hand.

"Glad to have you aboard, Mr Bastable."

"Thank you, sir. Glad to be aboard. I'm sorry I'm late, but . . ."

"I know, they shifted us to make way for that damned Russian freighter. You haven't delayed us. We're still giving our registration particulars a lick of paint and our passengers haven't arrived yet." He pointed to where a flight of six steps led to a door in the stern of the bridge. "Your cabin's through there. You mess with Mr Barry this voyage, but you'll have your own quarters as soon as we drop the passengers. We don't often carry many—though we've deck passengers coming aboard at Saigon—and your cabin's the only one suitable. All right?"

"Thank you, sir."

"Good."

I hefted my bag.

"Cabin's on the right," said Korzeniowski. "Mine's directly ahead and the passengers'—what will be yours—is on the left. I think Barry's expecting you. See you in fifteen minutes. Hoping to cast off, then."

I climbed the companionway and opened the connecting door to find myself in a short passage with the three doors leading off it. The walls were of plain grey colour, chipped and scored. I knocked on the door on my right.

"Enter."

Inside a tall, thin man with a great shock of red hair was sitting in his underclothes on the unmade bottom bunk. He was pouring himself a generous measure of gin. As I entered he looked up and nodded sociably. "Bastable? I'm Barry. Drink?" He extended the bottle then, as if remembering his manners, offered me the glass.

I smiled. "Bit early for me. I'm on the top bunk, eh?"

"Afraid so. Not what you're used to, probably, after the *Loch Etive.*"

"It suits me."

"You'll find a couple of uniforms in the locker, yonder. Marlowe was about your size, luckily. You can stow your other gear there, too. I heard about your fight. Good for you. This is a whole bloody ship of misfits. Not too strong on formal discipline, but we work hard and the skipper's one of the best."

"I liked him," I said. I began to put my gear in the locker and then took out a crumpled uniform. Barry was dragging on his trousers and a jersey.

"One of the best," he repeated. He finished his drink and carefully put bottle and glass away. "Well, I think I heard the passengers come aboard. We can leave at last. See you on the bridge when we let go."

As he opened the door to leave I glimpsed the back of one of the passengers entering the opposite cabin. A woman. A woman in a dark, heavy travelling coat. It was odd that Captain Korzeniowski should take on passengers. He didn't seem the type to welcome groundmen. But then it was likely that *The Rover* was glad to make any extra profit she could. Ships like her ran on a very narrow margin.

A short while later I joined the captain and Mr Barry on the bridge. Height and Steering Coxswains were at their controls and the wireless telephone operator was crouched in his cubbyhole in contact with the main traffic building, waiting to be told when we could let slip from our mast.

I looked through the wrap-round window of the bridge at all the fine ships. Our little freighter seemed so out of place here that I would be very glad to get away.

Captain Korzeniowski picked up a speaking tube. "Captain to all engines. Make ready."

A second later I heard the grumble of the diesels as their engineers began to warm them up.

The order came through from ground control. We could leave.

The captain took his position in the bow and peered down so that he could see the main mooring chains and the gangway. Barry went to the annunciator and stood by with the tube in his hand. The bosun stood halfway down the companionway to the embarkation platform, his body bisected by the deck of the bridge.

"Gangway withdrawn," said the captain. "Close and seal embarkation doors, bosun."

The bosun relayed this order to an unseen man below. There were noises, thumps, shouts. Then the bosun's head appeared on the companionway again. "All ready to slip, sir."

"Let slip." The captain straightened his back and drove both hands into the pockets of his jacket, his cheroot clamped between his teeth.

"Let slip below," said Barry into the tube.

There was a jerk as we were released by the mast. "All cables free."

"All cables free, below," said Barry.

The mooring cables snapped away and we were released into the air.

"Engines full astern."

Barry adjusted a switch. "All engines full astern." He was speaking now to the engineers crouched in their outside nacelles, nursing their diesels.

The ship shuddered and bucked slightly as the engines backed her away from the mast.

"Two hundred and fifty feet, Height Coxswain," said the captain, still peering through the bow observation port.

"Two hundred and fifty, sir." The coxswain spun his great metal wheel.

Slowly we crawled into the sky, our bow tilting upward slightly as the Elevator Coxswain operated his controls, adjusting the tailplanes.

And for the first time I had a sense of loss. I felt I was leaving behind everything I had come to understand about this world of the 1970s, embarking on what for me would be a fresh voyage of discovery. I felt a bit like one of the ancient Elizabethan navigators who had set off to look for the other side of the planet.

Croydon Airpark dropped behind us and we cruised over the fields of Kent towards the coast, gradually rising to a height of a thousand feet, moving at something under fifty miles an hour. The ship responded surprisingly well and I began to realise that there was more to *The Rover* than I had realised. I was learning not to judge an airship by her appearance. Primitive though her controls were, she flew smoothly and steadily and was almost stately in her progress through the sky. Barry, whom I had taken for a drunkard at the end of an unsavoury career, proved an efficient officer and I was to discover he drank heavily only when he was not in the air. I hoped that my stiff manner did not make my fellow officers think me a bit of a prig.

During the first day and night of our journey the passengers failed to emerge from their cabin. This did not strike me as particularly eccentric. They could be suffering from airsickness or perhaps they had no desire to go anywhere. After all, there were no promenade decks or kinemas on *The Rover*. If one wished to walk the length of the ship and see anything but the cargo stacked in semi-darkness, one had to go out onto the outside catwalks and cling to the rails for fear of being blown overboard.

I performed my duties with enthusiasm, if awkwardly at first, anxious to show Captain Korzeniowski that I was keen. I think both the skipper, Barry and the crew understood this and I soon found I was beginning to relax.

By the time we were over the bright blue waters of the Mediterranean and heading for Jerusalem, our first port of call, I had started to get the feel of *The Rover*.

She had to be treated gently and with what I can only describe as 'grace'. Handled in this way, she would do almost anything you asked of her. This may seem sentimental and foolish, but there was a sense of affection on that ship—a sense of humanity which extended to crew and craft alike.

But still I didn't see the passengers. They took their meals in their cabin and not in the little mess next to the galley where officers and ratings ate. It began to seem that they were shy of being seen, save by Captain Korzeniowski or Mr Barry, both of whom visited them occasionally.

We had no-one on board who was specifically a Navigator or Meteorological Officer. These duties were shared between the skipper, Barry and myself. The night before we arrived at Jerusalem, I had taken the dog watch and was checking our course against our charts and instruments when the telephone operator wandered in and started up a conversation. At length he said:

"What do you make of our passengers, Bastable?"

I shrugged. "I don't make anything of them, Johnson. I've only had a glimpse of one of them. A woman."

"I think they're refugees," Johnson said. "The old man says they're getting off at Brunei."

"Really. Not the safest spot in the world. Haven't they had bandit trouble there?"

"Terrorists of some kind. Well-organised, I gather. I heard the Germans and Japanese are backing them. Want some of our colonies, I shouldn't wonder."

"There are agreements. They wouldn't dare."

Johnson laughed. "You are a bit green, you know, Bastable. There's trouble brewing all over the East. Nationalism, old man. India, China, South East Asia. People are getting worried."

Johnson was a pessimist who relished such prospects. I took everything he said with a pinch of salt.

"I shouldn't be surprised if our passengers aren't countrymen of the old man. Polish exiles. Or even Russian anarchists, eh?"

I laughed aloud. "Come off it, Johnson. The skipper would have nothing to do with that sort of thing."

Johnson shook his head in mock reproof. "Oh dear, oh dear, Bastable. You *are* green. Sorry to have interrupted." He sauntered out of the bridge. I smiled and dismissed his bantering. He was plainly trying to agitate me. The sort of joke which is often played on 'new boys' on board any ship. Still, the passengers did seem anxious to keep themselves to themselves.

Next morning we moored at Jerusalem and I changed into my whites before seeing to the cargo, which was mainly boxes of farming machinery being delivered to the Palestinian Jewish immigrants. It was hot and dry and there was some confusion over two boxes which they had been expecting and which hadn't arrived.

Since I hadn't joined the ship until the cargo had all been taken on, I sent someone to find the captain. While I waited I bought an English-language newspaper from the boy who was selling them around the airpark. I glanced at it casually. The only real news concerned a bomb explosion at the house of Sir George Brown a few days earlier. Luckily Sir George had been away and a servant had been the sole person slightly hurt. But the papers were understandably upset by the outrage. The words *Freedom for the Colonies* had been scrawled on the wall of the house. The whole thing was plainly the work of fanatics and I wondered what kind of madmen could consider such means worthwhile. There were six or eight photographs of people suspected of being connected with the murder attempt, among them the notorious Count Rudolph von Dutchke who had long since been chased out of his German homeland and had, until the bombing, been thought to be in hiding in Denmark. Why a Prussian nobleman should turn against his own kind and all the ideals of his upbringing, nobody could understand.

Eventually the captain arrived and began to sort out the confusion. I folded the newspaper in my back pocket and continued with my duties.

The ways of Fate are strange indeed. It is hard to understand their workings—and I should know, for I have had enough experience of them, one way or another. What happened next is a fair example.

One of the cargo handlers had left a baling hook in a packing case and, as I moved into the hold, I caught my shirt against it, ripping it right across the back. It wasn't serious and I carried on with my job until the captain noticed what had happened.

"You'll get your back sunburned, if you're not careful," he said. "You'd better go and change, Mr. Bastable."

"If you think so, sir." I let one of our riggers keep an eye on the cargo and went back through the main passage between the holds and climbed the companionway up to the bridge and from there to my cabin. It was stinking hot in the little passage and all the doors of the cabins were open. For the first time, I got a clear look at the passengers as I passed. I couldn't stop and gape at them, though it took a considerable effort of will not to do so. I went into my own cabin and closed the door.

I was shaking as I sat down on the lower bunk and slowly removed the folded newspaper from my pocket. I had seen a man and a woman in the passenger cabin. The woman I had not recognised, but the face of the man was all too familiar. I opened the newspaper and looked again at the photographs of the anarchists wanted in connection with the attempt on Sir George Brown's life. My brain seething with a hundred different thoughts I looked hard at one of the photographs. There was no doubt about it. The tall, handsome man I had seen in the cabin was Count Rudolph von Dutchke the notorious anarchist and assassin!

Tears came into my eyes as the implications of this revelation dawned on me.

The kindly old airship skipper who had impressed me so much as a man of character and integrity, into whose hands I had so willingly put my fate, was himself at very least a Socialist sympathiser!

I was overwhelmed by a profound sense of betrayal. How could I have misjudged someone so badly?

I should, of course, contact the authorities and warn them at once. But how could I leave the ship without arousing suspicion? Doubtless all the officers and every member of the crew were of the same desperate persuasion as their captain. It was unlikely that I would reach the police in Jerusalem alive. And yet it was my duty to try.

Time must have passed rapidly while I carried on this debate with myself for, suddenly, I felt the ship lurch and I realised that we had already let slip from the mooring mast.

I was aloft, helpless now to do anything, in a ship full of dangerous and fanatical men who would certainly stop at nothing to silence me if they realised I suspected them.

With a groan I buried my head in my hands.

What a fool I had been to trust Dempsey—evidently, now, one of the same gang! I put it down to the fact that I had been badly disorientated after giving in my resignation.

The door opened suddenly and I jumped nervously. It was Barry. He was smiling. I looked at him in horror. How could he disguise his true nature so well?

"What's the matter, old chap?" he asked blandly. "Touch of the sun? The old man sent me to see if you were all right."

"Who—?" I spoke with great effort. "The—the passengers—why are they aboard?" I wanted to hear him give me an answer which would prove his and Captain Korzeniowski's innocence.

He looked at me in surprise for a moment and then said: "What—them across the passage? Why they're just old friends of the skipper's. He's doing them a favour."

"A favour?"

"That's right. Look here, you'd better lie down for a bit. You should have worn a hat, you know. Would you like a drop of something strong to pull you round?" He moved towards his locker.

How could he act so casually? I could only suppose that a life led so long beyond the bounds of the Law created an attitude of indifference both to the suffering caused to others and the corruption in one's own soul.

What chance had I against such men as Barry?

## BOOK THREE

### THE OTHER SIDE OF THE COIN—
### THE TABLES TURNED—ENTER THE
### WARLORD OF THE AIR—AND EXIT
### THE TEMPORAL EXCURSIONIST....

## CHAPTER I

### General O. T. Shaw

AS I LAY there in the cabin thinking back over the events of the past few days, I realised how Cornelius Dempsey, and later his compatriots in crime, had come to believe I was one of them. Seen from their perspective, my attack on Reagan had been an attack on the kind of authority he represented. Several hints had been dropped and, in misinterpreting them, I had allowed myself to be sucked into this appalling situation.

'We are both outcasts, in our way,' Captain Korzeniowski had said. Only now was I aware of the significance of those words! He thought me as desperate a character as himself! A Socialist! An Anarchist, even!

But then it began to dawn on me that I was in the perfect position to win back my honour—for every disgrace to be forgotten—to ensure that I was reinstated in the service I loved.

For they did not suspect me. They thought me one of themselves, still. If I could somehow seize control of the ship and force it to turn back to the British Air Port, I could then deliver the lot of them to the police. I should become a hero (not that I wanted honours for their own sake) and almost certainly I would be asked to rejoin my regiment. And then in my mind's eye I saw Captain Korzeniowski's face, his steady eyes, and I felt a dreadful pang. Was I to deliver this man into captivity? A man who had befriended me? A man who seemed so decent on the surface?

I hardened my heart. That was why he had managed to remain at liberty for so long—because he *seemed* so decent. He was a devil. Doubtless he had deceived many others in his long career of anarchy and crime, fooling them as he had fooled me.

I stood up, moving stiffly as if under the power of a mesmerist. I walked to Barry's locker where I knew he kept a large service revolver. I opened the locker. I took out the revolver and made sure that it was loaded. I tucked it into my belt and put on my jacket so that the gun was hidden.

Then I sat down again and tried to make a plan.

Our next port of call was Kandahar in Afghanistan. Although nominally allied to Britain, Afghanistan was notoriously fickle in her loyalties. In Kandahar there were Russians, Germans, Turks and Frenchmen, all conspiring to win that mountainous state to their side, all playing what Mr Kipling calls the Great Game of politics and intrigue. Even if I was able to leave the ship, there was no certainty that I should find a sympathetic ear in Kandahar. What then? Force the ship to turn back to Jerusalem? There were difficulties there, too. No, I must wait until we had let slip from Kandahar airpark and were on our way to the third port of call —Lahore, in British India.

So, until Kandahar was behind us, I must continue to try to act normally. Reluctantly, I replaced Barry's revolver in his locker. I drew a deep breath, tried to relax my features, and went up onto the bridge.

How I managed to deceive my new 'friends' I shall never know. I carried out my normal duties over the next few days and was as efficient as ever. Only in conversation with Korzeniowski, Barry or the others did I have difficulty. I simply could not bring myself to speak casually with them. They thought that I was still suffering some slight effects from the sun and were sympathetic. If I had not discovered them for what they were, I should have believed that their concern was genuine. Perhaps it was genuine—but they thought they were concerned for the well-being of one of their own.

Kandahar was reached—a walled city of bleak stone buildings which had not changed since my own day—and then we had left it. The tension within me increased. Again I availed myself of Barry's revolver. I checked the charts assiduously, waiting for the moment when we had crossed the border and arrived in India (which was now, of course, completely under British rule). Within a day we should be in Lahore. Feigning sickness, once more, I remained in my cabin and in my mind sketched out the final details of my plan.

I had ensured that none of the crew members nor the officers carried weapons as a rule. My plan depended on this fact.

The hours ticked by. We were due to moor at Lahore at noon. At eleven o'clock I left my cabin and went on to the bridge.

Captain Korzeniowski was standing with his back to the door, staring down through wisps of cloud at the brown, sun-beaten plains drifting past below us. Barry was at the computer, working out the best path of approach to Lahore airpark. The telephone operator was bent over his apparatus. Height and Steering Coxes were studying their controls. Nobody saw me as I entered silently and drew the revolver from my belt, holding it behind my back.

"Everything clear for Lahore?" I said.

Barry looked up, frowning. "Hello, Bastable. Feeling better?"

"Absolutely top-hole," I said. There was a funny note to my voice which even I heard.

Barry's frown darkened. "Splendid," he said. "If you feel like resting a bit longer. There's three quarters of an hour at least before we moor . . ."

"I'm fine. I just wanted to make sure we do get to Lahore."

Korzeniowski turned, smiling. "Why shouldn't we? Have you seen something in your tea-cup?"

"Not my tea-cup. . . . I'm afraid you've been under a misapprehension about me, captain."

"Have I?" He raised his eyebrows and continued to puff on his pipe. His coolness maddened me. I revealed the gun in my hand. I cocked the hammer. "Yes," he said, without changing his tone or his expression. "I think you may be right. More than a touch of the sun, mm?"

"Nothing to do with the sun, captain. I trusted you —trusted you all. I suppose it isn't your fault—after all, you thought I was one of you. 'Temperamentally, at least', to quote your friend Dempsey. But I'm not. I made the mistake of thinking you decent men—and you made the mistake of thinking me a villain like yourselves. Ironic, isn't it?"

"Very." Still Korzeniowski's demeanour did not alter. But Barry was looking startled, glancing first at my face and then at the captain's, as if he thought we had both gone mad.

"You know what I'm talking about, of course," I said to Korzeniowski.

"I must admit I'm not sure, Bastable. If you want my frank opinion, I think you're having a fit of some kind. I hope you don't intend to hurt anyone."

"I'm extremely rational," I said. "I have discovered what you and your crew are, captain. I mean to take this ship to Lahore—the military section of the airpark —and there deliver it and you up to the authorities."

"For smuggling, perhaps?"

"No, captain—for treason. You pointed out to me that you were a British subject. For harbouring wanted criminals—your two passengers. Dutchke and the girl.

You see, I know who they are. And I know what you are—anarchist sympathisers, at best. At worst, well . . ."

"I see that I did misjudge you, my boy." Korzeniowski removed the pipe from his mouth. "I did not want you to find out about our passengers because I wanted you to share no part of the burden—in case we were caught. My sympathies do, in fact, lie with people like Count Dutchke and Miss Persson—she is the count's lady friend. They are what I think of as moderate radicals. You think they had something to do with the bombings?"

"The newspapers do. The police do."

"That is because they will brand everyone with the same iron," Korzeniowski said. "As you doubtless do."

"You can't talk your way out of this, captain." My hand had begun to shake and for a moment I felt a weakening of my resolve. "I know you for the hypocrite you are."

Korzeniowski shrugged. "This is silly. But I agree—it is also ironic. I thought you, well, neutral, at least."

"Whatever else I am, captain, I am a patriot," I said.

"I think that I am that, too," he smiled. "I believe most strongly in the British ideal of justice. But I should like to see that ideal spread a little further than the shores of one small island. I should like to see it put into practice the world over. I admire what Britain stands for in many ways. But I do not admire what she has done to her colonies, for I have had some experience of what it is to live under foreign rule, Bastable."

"Russia's conquest of Poland is scarcely the same as Britain's administration of India," I said.

"I see no great difference, Bastable." He sighed. "But you must do what you think right. You have the gun. And the man with the gun is always right, eh?"

I refused to be drawn into this trap. Like most Slavs, he had proved to be a superb logic-splitter.

Barry broke in, his Irish brogue seemingly thicker than before. "Conquest—administration—or, in the Americans' terms, the loan of 'advisors'—it's all the same, Bastable, me boy. And it has the same vice at its root— the vice of greed. I've yet to see a colony that is better off than the nation which colonised it. Poland—Ire- land—Siam ..."

"Like most fanatics," I pointed out coolly, "you share at least one characteristic with children—you want ev- erything *now*. All improvements take time. You cannot make the world perfect overnight. Things are con- siderably better for more people today than they were in my—in the early years of this century, for instance."

"In some ways," Korzeniowski said. "But the old evils remain. And will continue until those who have the most power are made to understand that they *are* promoting evil."

"And you would make them understand by exploding bombs, murdering ordinary men and women, agitating ignorant natives to take part in risings in which they are bound to come off worst? That is not my idea of people who oppose evil."

"Nor is it mine, in those terms," said Korzeniowski.

"Dutchke has never let off a bomb in his life!" said Barry.

"He has given his blessing to those who do. It is the same thing," I countered.

I heard a small sound behind me and tried to back away to see what caused it. But then I felt something press forcefully into my ribs. A hand appeared and covered the cylinder of my revolver and a quiet, slightly amused voice said:

"I suppose you are right, Herr Bastable. When all is said and done, we are what we are. Our temperaments are such that we support one side or the other. And, I'm afraid, your side is not doing too well today."

Before I could think, he had taken the gun from my hand and I turned to confront the cynically smiling face of the arch-anarchist himself. Behind him stood a pretty girl dressed in a long, black travelling coat. Her short, dark hair framed her heart-shaped, serious little face and she stared at me curiously with steady, grey eyes which reminded me immediately of Korzeniowski's.

"This is my daughter, Una Persson," said the captain from over my shoulder. "You know Count von Dutchke already, of course."

Once again I had failed to fulfill an ambition in this world of the future. I became convinced that I was doomed never to succeed in anything I set out to do. Was it simply because I was a man existing in a period of history not his own? Or, faced with similar situations in my own time, would I have bungled my opportunities as I had these?

This was the drift of my thoughts as I sat in my cabin, a prisoner, as the ship came and went from Lahore and began heading for its next destination, which was Calcutta. After Calcutta came Saigon where the 'deck passengers' were due to come aboard, and then Brunei, where Dutchke and his beautiful woman friend were bound (doubtless to join the terrorists seeking to end British rule there). After Brunei we were due to pay a call at Canton, where we would put off the pilgrims who were our deck passengers (or more likely terrorist friends of Korzeniowski's!) and then start back, via Manila and Darwin. I wondered which of these ports I should visit before the anarchists decided what to do with me. Probably they were trying to decide that now. It should not be difficult to claim that I had been lost overboard at some convenient point.

Barry brought my food in, his own revolver once again in his possession. So distorted was his point of view that he seemed genuinely sorrowful that I had turned out to be a 'traitor'. Certainly he seemed more sympathetic than angry. I still found it hard to see Barry and Korzeniowski as villains and once I asked Barry if Una Persson, the captain's daughter, was in some way a hostage for the captain's good behaviour. Barry laughed at this and shook his head. "No, me boy. She's her father's daughter, that's all there is to that!" But it was evidently the connection—why *The Rover* had been chosen as the vessel in which they had made their escape from Britain. It also proved to me that the captain's moral sensibilities must be stunted, to say the least, if he allowed his daughter to share a cabin with a man to whom she was evidently not married (where was Mr Persson? I wondered—doubtless another anarchist who *had* been apprehended). Plainly I did not have much chance of living more than a few hours longer.

I had one hope. Johnson, the telephone operator, had certainly not been in the know about Dutchke's identity. Although he might have other reasons for choosing to serve aboard *The Rover*, he was not the committed socialist the others were. Perhaps I could bribe Johnson in some way? Or offer him help, if he needed it, if he would help me now. But how was I to contact Johnson? And if I did contact him, would he not fall under suspicion and be unable to get a telephone message out to a British airpark?

I stared through the tiny porthole of my cabin. When we had berthed at Lahore, Dutchke had kept me at gunpoint so that I might not shout out or drop a message through. I could see nothing but grey clouds going on and on for miles. And all I could hear was the steady roar of *The Rover*'s cumbersome engines, bearing me, it seemed, closer and closer to my doom.

At Calcutta, Dutchke once again joined me in my cabin, his revolver pointing at my breast. I glanced out at the sunshine, at a distant city I had known and loved in my own time but now could not recognise. How could these anarchists say that British rule was bad when it had done so much to modernise India? I put this to Dutchke who only laughed.

"Do you know how much a pair of good boots costs in England?"

"About ten shillings," I said.

"And here?"

"Probably less."

"About thirty shillings in Calcutta—if you are an Indian. About five shillings if you are a European. Europeans, you see, control the bootmaking trade. While they are able to buy from the source, the Indian has to buy from a shop. Retail shops need to charge thirty shillings and this is what the average Indian earns in a month. Food costs more in Delhi than it does in Manchester, but the Indian workman earns a quarter of what the English workman earns. You know why this is?"

"No." It seemed a pack of lies to me.

"Because Britain's prices and incomes are maintained artificially, at the expense of her colonies. All trade agreements favour her. She sets the price at which she buys. She controls the means of production so that the price remains stable no matter how the market fluctuates. The Indian starves so that the Briton may feast. It is the same in all colonies and 'possessions' and protectorates, no matter how it is dressed up."

"But there are hospitals, welfare programmes, there is a dole system," I said. "The Indian does not starve."

"True—he is kept alive. It is silly to let your pool of available labour die altogether, for you never know when you may next need it. Slaves represent wealth, do they not?"

I refused to rise to this sort of inflammatory stuff. I was not sure his economics were particularly sound, for one thing, and for another I was certain that he saw everything through the distorting glass of his own mind.

"All I know is that the average Indian is better off than he was in 1900," I said. "Better off than many English people were in those days."

"You have seen only the cities. Do you know that Indians are only allowed to come to the cities if they have permission from the government? They must carry passes which say they have a job here. If they have no job, they are returned to the countryside where they live in villages where schools, hospitals and all the other advantages of British rule are few and far between.

This sort of system applies throughout Africa and the East. It has been developed over the years and now even applies to some European colonies—Poland under the Russians, Bohemia under the Germans."

"I know the system," I said. "It is not inhumane. It is merely a means of controlling the flow of labour, of stopping the cities from turning into the slums they once were. Everyone benefits."

"It is a system of slavery," said the aristocratic anarchist. "It is unjust. It leads to further erosions of liberty. You support tyrants, my friend, when you support such a system."

I smiled and shook my head. "Ask the Indian man in the street how he feels. He will tell you he is satisfied, I am sure."

"Because he knows no better. Because the British conspire to teach him just a little—enough to confuse his mind and let him swallow their propaganda, no more. It is strange that their educational spending remains the same, when certain other forms of 'welfare' spending go up to meet the demand. Thus have you broken the spirit of those you have conquered. You are the ones who speak complacently of free enterprise, of a man standing on his own feet, of 'bettering himself' by his own efforts—and then are horrified when those you colonise resent your patronage, your 'system of controlling the flow of labour'. Bah!"

"I might remind you," I said, "that, compared with seventy years ago, this world has a stability it has previously never known. There have been no major wars. There has been a hundred years of peace throughout most of the world. Is that an evil?"

"Yes—for your stability has been achieved at the expense of the pride of others. You have destroyed souls, not bodies, and in my opinion that is an evil of the worst kind."

"Enough of this!" I cried impatiently. "You're boring me, Count von Dutchke. You should feel satisfied that you have defeated my plans. I'll listen no longer. I regard myself as a decent man—a humane man—indeed, a liberal man—but your kind makes me want to—want to—well, I had better not say. . . ." I controlled my temper.

"You see!" Dutchke laughed. "I am the voice of your conscience. That which you refuse to hear. And you are so determined not to hear it that you would wipe out anyone who tries to make you hear! You are so typical of all those 'decent', 'humane' and 'liberal' men who hold two thirds of the world in slavery." He gestured with his pistol. "It is strange how all authoritarians automatically assume that the libertarian wishes to impose his own views on them when all he actually wants to do is to appeal to the authoritarian's better nature. But I suppose you authoritarians can only see things in your own terms."

"You cannot confuse me with your arguments. At least give me the privilege of spending my last hours in silence."

"As you wish."

Until we let slip from the mooring mast, he said little, save to mutter something about the 'dignity of man' having come to mean nothing more than the 'arrogance of the conqueror'. But I shut my ears to his ravings. It was he who was arrogant, in seeking to foist his revolutionary notions onto me.

During the next part of the voyage I made desperate efforts to contact Johnson, saying that I was sick of my food being brought by Barry and I would enjoy seeing a face other than his.

Instead, they sent me the captain's daughter. Her grace and her beauty were such that I could scarcely scowl at her as I had at the others. I tried, once or twice, to find out from her what her father intended to do with me but she said he was still 'puzzling it over'. Would she help me? I asked directly. She seemed astonished at this and made no reply of any sort, but left the cabin in some haste.

At Saigon—I could tell it must be Saigon by the glitter of gilded temples in the distance—I heard the babble of the Indo-Chinese pilgrims taking their places in the space alloted for them amongst the bales of cargo. I did not envy them those hot, cramped quarters, but, of course, they were lucky—if they were genuine Buddhist pilgrims—to get an airship passage at all.

Once again—although Saigon was a 'free' port, under American patronage—I was guarded vigilantly by a Count Rudolph von Dutchke who seemed less sure of himself than on the previous occasion we had met. He was definitely ill at ease and it occurred to me that the American authorities might have had some wind of *The Rover*'s mission and were asking awkward questions. We certainly left in what seemed to be a hurry and took the air scarcely three hours after we had moored and refueled, the engines going full out.

Later that evening I heard from across the little passage the sounds of voices raised in argument. I recognised the voices as belonging to Dutchke, the captain, Barry and Una Persson—and there seemed to be another voice, softer and very calm, which I did not recognise.

I heard a few words—'Brunei'—'Canton'—'Japanese' —'Shantung'—mainly names of places which I recognised, but I could not guess the nature of the argument.

A day passed and I was brought food only once—by Una Persson who apologised that it was a cold meal. She looked strained and rather worried. I asked her if anything were wrong. It was politeness which made me ask. She gave me a baffled look and a brief, bewildered smile. "I'm not sure," was all she said before leaving and locking my door on the outside as usual.

It was midnight, when we must have been well on our way to Brunei, that I heard the first shot. At first I thought it was a sound made by one of the engines, but I knew at once that I was wrong.

I got up, still dressed in my clothes, and stumbled

to the door, pressing my ear against it and listening hard. Now I heard more shots—shouting—the sound of running feet. What on Earth was happening? Had the villains fallen out amongst themselves? Or had we landed without realising it and taken on a boarding party of British or American police?

I went to the porthole. We were still airborne, flying high over the China Sea, if my guess were right.

The sounds of fighting went on for at least another half-an-hour. Then there were no more shots, but voices raised in angry exchange. Then the voices died. I heard footfalls in the passage, I heard the key turn in the lock on my door.

Light burst in and half-blinded me.

I blinked at the tall figure which stood framed in the opening, a revolver in one hand, his other hand on the door-knob. He was dressed in flowing Asiatic robes but his handsome face was distinctly Eurasian—a mixture of Chinese and English if I were not mistaken.

"Good morning, Lieutenant Bastable," he said in perfect Oxford English. "I am General O. T. Shaw and this ship is now under my command. I believe you have some flying experience. I should be very grateful if you would allow me to avail myself of that experience."

My jaw dropped in stupefied astonishment.

I knew that name. Who did not? The man who addressed me was known far and wide as the fiercest of the bandit chieftains who plagued the Central Government of the Chinese Republic. This was Shuo Ho Ti—Warlord of Chihli!

## CHAPTER II

### The Valley of the Morning

MY FIRST THOUGHT was that I had been lifted out of the frying pan into the fire. But then I realised that it was the habit of many Chinese warlords to hold their European prisoners to ransom. With luck, my government might pay for my release. I smiled to myself when I thought that Korzeniowski and Company had innocently taken on board a gang of rascals even more villainous than themselves. Here was the best irony of them all.

General O. T. Shaw (or Shuo Ho Ti as he styled himself for the sake of his Chinese followers) had built himself an army of bandits, renegades and deserters so big that it controlled large areas of the provinces of Chihli, Shantung and Kiangsu, giving Shaw a stranglehold on the routes between Peking and Shanghai. He charged such an extortionate sum as a 'toll' on trains and motors which came through his territory that trade and communications between the two cities was now conducted almost wholly by airship—and not every airship was safe if it flew low enough to be shot at by Shaw's cannon. The Central Government was powerless against him and too fearful of seeking assistance from the foreigners who administered large parts of China which were not in the Republic. For the foreigners—Russians and Japanese for the most part—might make it their excuse to occupy that territory and refuse to leave. This was what gave Shaw—and warlords like him—his power.

I had been taken aback at meeting such a famous and romantic figure in the flesh. But now I managed to speak.

"Why—why should you want me to fly the ship?"

The tall Eurasian smoothed his straight, black hair and looked more like a devil than ever as he replied softly: "I'm afraid Mr Barry is dead. Captain Korzeniowski is wounded. You are the only person qualified to do the job."

"Barry dead?" I should have been exultant, but instead I felt a sense of loss.

"My men reacted hastily when they saw he had a gun. They are frightened, you see, of being so high in the air. They feel that if they die the spirits of the upper regions—devils all—will capture their souls. They are ignorant, superstitious men, my followers."

"And how badly is Captain Korzeniowski hurt?"

"A head wound. Not a serious one. But, naturally, he is very dizzy and not up to commanding the ship."

"His daughter—and Count Dutchke?"

"They are locked in their cabin, with the captain."

"Johnson?"

"He was last seen on the outer catwalk. I believe he

fell overboard during a fight with some of my men."

"My God," I muttered. "My God." I felt sick. "This is piracy. Murder. I can hardly believe it."

"It is all of those things, I regret to say," said Shaw. I recognised the soft voice now, of course. I had heard it earlier when they had been arguing in the opposite cabin. "But we do not wish to kill any more, now that we have control of the ship and can fly it to Shantung. None of this would have happened if your Count Dutchke had not insisted we go to Brunei, even though I warned him that the British knew he was aboard *The Rover* and would be waiting for him there."

"How did you know that?"

"It is the duty of a leader to know everything he can and so benefit his people accordingly," was the rather ambiguous reply.

"And what will you do for me if I agree to help you?" I asked.

"It is what we shall do to the others which might interest you more. We shall refrain from torturing them to death. This might not impress you, however, since they are enemies of yours. But they *are*" (he lifted his right eyebrow sardonically) "fellow white men."

"Whatever they are—and I've nothing but contempt for them—I wouldn't want them tortured by your ruffians!"

"If all goes well, nobody will be harmed." Shaw uncocked his revolver and lowered it, but he did not put it back in the holster at his hip. "I assure you that I do not enjoy killing and I give you my word that the lives of all aboard *The Rover* will be spared—*if* we reach The Valley of the Morning safely."

"Where is this valley?"

"In Shantung. It is my headquarters. We will guide you when you reach Wuchang. It is expedient that we reach there quickly. Originally we meant to go to Canton and move overland from there, but someone had telephoned that we were aboard—Johnson, I suppose —and it became obvious we must go directly to our base, without pause. If Count Dutchke had not objected to this plan, all trouble might have been averted."

So Johnson had been on my side! In trying to save me and warn the authorities of all that was happening aboard *The Rover,* he had brought about this disaster and caused his own death.

It was horrible. Johnson had, in effect, died trying to save me. And now his killer was asking me to fly him to safety. But if I did not, others would die, too. Though some of them deserved death, they did not deserve to have it served to them in the manner which Shaw had hinted at. I sighed deeply and my shoulders sagged as I made my reply. All heroics seemed pointless now.

"I have your word that we shall not be harmed if I do as you wish?"

"You have my word."

"Very well, General Shaw. I'll fly your damned airship."

"That's very decent of you, old man," said Shaw beaming and clapping me on the shoulder. He holstered his revolver.

When I arrived on the bridge my horror was increased by the sight of the blood spattered everywhere on the floor, the bulkheads, the instruments. At least one person had been shot at close range—probably poor Barry. The coxswains were at their positions. They looked pale and shocked. Beside each coxswain stood two Chinese bandits, their bodies criss-crossed with bandoliers of bullets, their belts bristling with knives and smallarms. I had never in my life seen such a murderous gang as Shaw's followers. No attempt had been made to clean the mess and charts and log-tables were scattered about the bridge, some of them soaked in blood.

"I can do nothing until all this is cleaned up," I said bleakly. Shaw said something in Cantonese and, very reluctantly, two of the bandits left the bridge to return with buckets and mops. As they worked, I inspected the instruments to make sure they were still in working order. Apart from some dents caused by bullets, nothing was badly damaged except the telephone which looked to me as if it had been scientifically destroyed, perhaps by Johnson himself before he had made a run for the outer catwalk.

At last the bandits finished. Shaw gestured towards the main controls. We were flying very low at not much more than three hundred feet—a dangerous height.

"Put her up to seven hundred and fifty feet, Height Coxswain," I said grimly. Without a word, the coxswain did as he was ordered. The ship tilted steeply and Shaw's eyes narrowed, his hand going to his holster, but then we levelled out. I found the appropriate charts for China and studied them.

"I think I can get us to Wuchang," I said. If necessary, we could always follow the railway line, but I doubted if Shaw was prepared to drop speed. He seemed anxious to get into his own territory by morning. "But before I begin, I want to be certain that Captain Korzeniowski and the others are still alive."

Shaw pursed his lips and gave me a hard look. Then he turned on his heel. "Very well. Follow me." Another order in Cantonese and a bandit fell into step behind me.

We reached the middle cabin and Shaw took a key from his belt, unlocking the door.

Three wretched faces stared up at us from the cabin. A crude bandage had been tied around Captain Korzeniowski's head. It was soaked in blood. His face was ashen and he looked much older than the last time I had seen him. He did not appear to recognise me. His daughter was cradling his head in her lap. Her hair was awry and she seemed to have been crying. She offered Shaw a glare of hatred and contempt. Dutchke saw us and looked away.

"Are you—all right?" I asked rather foolishly.

"We are not dead, Mr Bastable," Dutchke said bit-

terly, standing up and turning his back on us. "Is that what you meant?"

"I am trying to save your lives," I said, a little priggishly under the circumstances, but I wanted them to know that a chap of my sort was capable of generosity towards his enemies. "I'm going to fly this ship to—General—Shaw's base. He says he'll not kill any of us if I do that."

"His word's hardly to be trusted after what's happened tonight," said Dutchke. He gave a strange, harsh laugh. "Odd that you should find our politics so disgusting when you can throw in your lot cheerfully with him!"

"He's scarcely a politician," I pointed out. "Besides, it wouldn't matter who he was. He holds all the cards —save the one I'm playing now."

"Goodnight, Mr Bastable," said Una Persson, stroking

her father's head. "I think you mean well. Thank you."

Embarrassed I backed out of the cabin and returned to the bridge.

By morning we had reached Wuchang and Shaw was evidently much more relaxed than he had been during the night. He went so far as to offer me a pipe of opium which I instantly refused. In those days opium seemed pretty disgusting stuff—it shows you how much I've changed, eh?

Wuchang was quite a large city, but we passed it before it was properly awake, flying over terraced roofs, pagodas, little blue-roofed houses, while Shaw got his bearings and pointed out the direction in which we should go.

There is nothing like a Chinese sunrise. A great watery sun appeared over the horizon and the whole land was turned to soft tones of pink, yellow and orange as we approached a line of sand-coloured hills. I felt that we offended such beauty with our battered, noisy airship full of so many cutthroats of various nationalities.

Then we were flying over the hills themselves and Shaw told us to slow our speed. He issued more rapid orders in Cantonese and one of his men left the bridge and made for the ladder which would lead him onto the outer catwalk on the top of the hull. Plainly the man was to make some sort of signal that we were friendly.

Then, suddenly, we were over a valley. It was a deep, wide valley through which a river wound. It was a green, lush valley which seemed to have no business in that rocky landscape. I saw herds of cattle grazing. I saw small farmhouses, rice fields, pigs and goats.

"Is this the valley?" I asked.

Shaw nodded. "This is the Valley of the Morning. And look, Mr Bastable—there is my 'camp'. . . ."

He pointed ahead. I saw high, white buildings, separated by patches of greenery. I saw fountains splashing and nearby were the tiny figures of children at play.

Over this modern township there flew a large, crimson flag—doubtless Shaw's battle flag. I was astonished to see such a settlement in these wilds and even more astonished to learn that it was Shaw's headquarters. It seemed so peaceful, so civilised!

Shaw was grinning at me, wholly amused by my surprise.

"Not bad for a barbarian warlord, eh? We built it all ourselves. It has every amenity—and some which even London cannot boast."

I looked at Shaw through new eyes. Bandit, pirate, murderer he might be—but he must be something more than these to have built such a city in the Chinese wilderness.

"Haven't you read my publicity, Mr Bastable? Perhaps you haven't seen the *Shanghai Express* recently. They are calling me the Chinese Alexander! This is my Alexandria. This is Shawtown, Mr Bastable!" He was chuckling like a schoolboy, delighted at his own achievements. "I built it. I built it."

My first shock of amazement died away. "Perhaps you did," I murmured, "but you built it from the flesh and bones of those you have murdered and painted it with the same crimson blood which stains your flag."

"A rather rhetorical statement for you, Mr Bastable. As it happens, I am not normally much of a hand at murder. I'm a soldier, really. You appreciate the difference?"

"I appreciate the difference, but my experience has shown me that you are not anything more than a murderer, 'General' Shaw."

He laughed again. "We'll see, we'll see. Now—look over there. Do you recognise her? There—on the other side of the city? There!"

I saw her at last, her huge bulk moving gently in the wind, her mooring ropes holding her close to the ground. And I recognised her, sure enough.

"My God!" I exclaimed. "You've got the *Loch Etive!*"

"Yes," he said eagerly, again like a schoolboy who

has added a rather good new stamp to his collection.

"That's her name. She's to be my flagship. At this rate I'll soon have my own airfleet. What d'you think of that, Mr Bastable? Soon I'll control not only the ground, but the air as well. What a warlord I shall be! Something *of* a warlord, eh?"

I stared at his eager, glowing face and I could think of no reply. He was not mad. He was not naïve. He was not a fool. He was, in fact, one of the most intelligent men I had ever encountered. He baffled me absolutely.

He had thrown back his head and was laughing joyfully at his own cleverness—at his own wholly gargantuan act of cheek in stealing what was perhaps the finest and biggest aerial liner in the skies!

"Oh, Mr Bastable!" His half-Chinese features were still creased with mirth. "What larks, Mr Bastable! What larks!"

## CHAPTER III

### Chi'ng Che'eng Ta-Chia

THERE WERE NO MOORING masts on the flat space outside the city and so ropes had to be flung down to waiting men who manhandled the ship until the gondola touched the ground. Then cables and ropes were pegged into the earth, holding *The Rover* as, further away, the *Loch Etive* was held.

As we disembarked, under the suspicious gaze of Shaw's armed bandits, I expected to see coolies come hurrying up to strip the ship of its cargo, but the men who arrived were healthy, well-dressed fellows whom I first mistook for clerks or traders. Shaw had a word with them and they began to go aboard the airship, showing no subservience of the sort normally shown to bandit chieftains by their men. In fact the pirates who disembarked with their guns and knives and bandoliers, their ragged silks, sandles and beaded headbands, looked distinctly out of place here. Shortly after landing, they climbed into a large motor wagon and steamed away towards the far end of the valley. "They go to join the rest of the army," Shaw explained. "Chi'ng Che'eng Ta-Chia is primarily a civilian settlement."

I was helping Captain Korzeniowski, supporting one elbow while Una Persson supported the other. Dutchke strode moodily ahead of us as we moved towards the town. Korzeniowski was better today and his old intelligence had returned. Behind us streamed the crewmen of *The Rover*, looking about them in open amazement.

"What was that name you used?" I asked the 'General'.

"Chi'ng Che'eng Ta-Chia—it's hard to translate. The name of the city yonder."

"I thought you called it Shawtown."

He burst into laughter again, his great frame shaking, his hands on his hips. "My joke, Mr Bastable! The place is called—well—Democratic Dawn City, perhaps? Dawn City Belonging to Us All? Something like that. Call it Dawn City, if you like. In the Valley of the Dawn. The first city of the New Age."

"What New Age is that?"

"Shuo Ho Ti—his New Age. Do you want the translation of my Chinese name, Mr Bastable? It is 'One Who Makes Peace'—The Peacemaker."

"Now that isn't a bad joke at all," I said grimly as we strode over the grass towards the first tall, elegant buildings of Dawn City. "Considering that you've just murdered two English officers and stolen a British airship. How many people did you have to kill to get your hands on the *Loch Etive?*"

"Not many. You must meet my friend Ulianov—he will tell you that the ends justify the means."

"And what exactly are your ends?" I grew impatient

as Shaw flung an arm round my shoulders, his bland Oriental face beaming.

"First—the Liberation of China. Driving out all foreigners—Russians, Japanese, British, Americans, French —all of them."

"I doubt if you'll manage it," I said. "And even if you did, you'd probably starve. You need foreign money."

"Not really. Not really. Foreigners—particularly the British with their opium trade—ruined our economy in the first place. It will be hard to build it up again alone, but we shall do it."

I said nothing to this. His were evidently messianic dreams, not unlike those of old Sharan Kang—he believed himself much more powerful than he actually was. I almost felt sorry for him then. It would only take a fleet of His Majesty's aerial battleships to turn his whole dream into a nightmare. Now that he had committed acts of piracy against Great Britain he had become something more than a local problem to be dealt with by the Chinese authorities.

As if reading my thoughts, he said, "The passengers and crew of the *Loch Etive* make useful hostages, Mr Bastable. I doubt if we'll be attacked by your battleships immediately, eh?"

"Perhaps you're right. What are your plans *after* you have liberated all China?"

"The world, of course."

It was my turn to laugh. "Oh, I see."

He smiled a secret smile, then. "Do you know who lives in Dawn City, Mr Bastable?"

"How could I? Members of your government-to-be?"

"Some of those, yes. But Dawn City is a town of outlaws. There are exiles here from every oppressed country in the world. It is an international settlement."

"A town of criminals?"

"Some would call it that." We were now strolling through wide streets flanked by willows and poplars, grassy lawns and bright beds of flowers. From the open window of one of the houses drifted the sound of a violin playing Mozart. Shaw paused and listened, the crew of *The Rover* coming to a straggling halt behind us. "Beautiful, isn't it?"

"Very fine. A phonograph?"

"A man. Professor Hira. He's an Indian physicist. Because of his nationalist sympathies he was put in prison. My men helped him escape and now he is continuing his research in one of our laboratories. We have many laboratories—many new inventions. Tyrants hate original thinking. So the original thinkers are driven to Dawn City. We have scientists, philosophers, artists, journalists—even a few politicians."

"And plenty of soldiers," I said harshly.

"Yes, plenty of soldiers—lots of guns and stuff," he said vaguely as if slightly put out by my interruption.

"And it will all be wasted," said Dutchke suddenly, turning to look back at us. "Because you wish to control too much power, Shaw."

Shaw waved a languid hand. "I have been lucky in that, Rudy. I have the power. I must use it."

"Against fellow comrades. I was expected in Brunei. A revolt was planned. Without me there to lead it, it would have collapsed. It must have collapsed by now."

I stared at him. "You know each other?"

"Very well," Dutchke said angrily. "Too damn' well."

"Then you, too, are a socialist?" I said to Shaw.

Shaw shrugged. "I prefer the term communist, but names don't matter. That is Dutchke's trouble—he cares about names. I told you, Rudy, that the British authorities were waiting to arrest you, that the Americans already knew there was something suspicious about *The Rover* when you reached Saigon. Your telephone operator must have been sending out secret messages to them. But you wouldn't listen—and Barry and the telephone man died because of your obstinacy!"

"You had no right to take over the ship!" shouted the German count. "No right at all."

"If I had not, we should all be in some British jail by now—or dead."

Korzeniowski said weakly, "It's all over. Shaw has presented us with a *fait accompli* and there it is. But I wish you had better control over your men, Shaw. . . . Poor Barry wouldn't have shot you, you know that."

"*They* didn't know it. My army is a democratic army."

"If you're not careful they'll destroy you," Korzeniowski continued. "They serve you only because they consider you the best bandit in China. If you try to discipline them, you'll find them cutting your throat."

Shaw accepted this. He led the way up a concrete path towards a low pagoda-style building. "I do not intend to rely on them much longer. As soon as my air-fleet is ready . . ."

"Air-fleet!" snorted Dutchke. "Two ships?"

"Soon I'll have more," Shaw said confidently. "Many more."

We entered the cool gloom of a hallway. "It is old-fashioned to rely on armies, Rudy," Shaw went on. "I rely on science. We have many projects nearing fruition—and if Project NFB is successful, then I think I'll disband the army altogether."

"NFB?" Una Persson frowned. "What's that?"

Shaw laughed. "You are a physicist, Una—the last person I should tell anything to at this stage."

A European in a neat, white suit appeared in the hallway. He smiled at us in welcome. He had grey hair, a wrinkled face.

"Ah, Comrade Spender. Could you accommodate these people here for a while?"

"A pleasure, Comrade Shaw." The old man walked to a section of the blank wall and passed his hand across it. Instantly a series of rows of coloured lights appeared on the wall. Some of them were red, but most were blue. Comrade Spender studied the blue lights thoughtfully for a moment then turned back to us. "We have the whole of Section Eight free. One moment, I'll prepare the rooms." He touched a bank of blue lights and they changed to red. "It is done. All operating now."

"Thank you, Comrade Spender."

I wondered what this peculiar ritual could mean.

Shaw led us down a corridor with wide windows which looked out onto a forecourt in which several fountains were playing. The fountains were in the latest styles of architecture—not all entirely to my taste. We came to a door with a large figure 8 stencilled on it. Shaw pressed his hand against the numeral and said: "Open!" At once, the door slid upwards, disappearing into the ceiling. "You'll have to share rooms, I'm afraid," said Shaw. "Two of you in each room. There's everything you need and you can communicate any other wants by means of the telephones you'll find. Goodbye for now, gentlemen." He turned and the door slid down behind him. I went up to it and put my palm against it.

"Open!" I said.

As I expected, nothing happened. Somehow the door was keyed to recognise Shaw's hand and voice! This certainly was a city of scientific marvels!

After some discussion and a general pacing about and testing of the windows and doors, we realised there was no easy means of escape.

"You'd better share a room with me, I suppose," said Dutchke, tapping me on the shoulder. "Una and the Captain Korzeniowski can go next door." The crewmen were already entering their rooms, finding that the doors opened and shut on command.

"Very well," I said distastefully.

We entered our room and found that there were two beds in it, a writing desk, wardrobes, chests of drawers, bookshelves filled with a wide variety of fiction and non-fiction, a telephone communicator and something with a milky-blue surface which was oval in shape and unidentifiable. Our windows looked out onto a sweet-scented rose-garden, but the glass was unbreakable and the windows could only be opened wide enough to let in the air and the scent. Pale blue sleeping suits had been laid on the beds. Ignoring the suit, Rudolph von Dutchke flung himself on the bed fully clothed, turning his head and giving me a bleak smile.

"Well, Bastable, now that you've met a real, full-blooded revolutionary, I must look pretty pale in comparison, eh?"

I sat down on the edge of the bed and began to remove my boots, which were pinching. "You're all as bad," I said. "All that makes Shaw different from you is that his madness is that much grander—and a thousand times more foolish! At least you confined your activities to what was possible. He dreams of the impossible."

"That's what I like to think," Dutchke said seriously. "But there again—he's built Dawn City up a lot since I was here last. And one would have thought it impossible to steal a liner the size of the *Loch Etive*. And there's no doubting that his scientific gadgets—this whole apartment building, for instance—are in advance of anything which exists in the outside world." He frowned. "I wonder what Project NFB could be?"

"I don't care," I said. "My only wish is to get back to the civilisation I know—a sane world where people behave with a reasonable degree of decency!"

Dutchke smiled patronisingly. Then he sat up and stretched. "By God, I'm hungry! I wonder if we get any food?"

"Food," said a voice from nowhere. I watched, fascinated, as a face appeared in the milky-blue oval. It was a Chinese girl. She smiled and continued. "What would you like to eat, gentlemen? Chinese food—or European?"

"Let's have some Chinese food, by all means," said Dutchke without consulting me. "I'm very fond of it. What have you got?"

"We will send you a selection." The girl's face vanished from the screen.

A few moments later, while we were still recovering from that experience, a section of the wall opened to reveal an alcove in which sat a tray piled high with all kinds of Chinese delicacies. Eagerly Dutchke sprang up, seized the tray and placed it on our table.

Forgetting for an instant everything but the mouth-watering smell of the food, I began to eat, wondering, not for the first time, if this were not perhaps some fantastically detailed dream induced by Sharan Kang's drugs.

## CHAPTER IV

### Vladimir Ilyitch Ulianov

AFTER EATING I washed, dressed myself in the sleeping suit and climbed beneath the quilt covering the bed. The bed was the most comfortable I had ever slept in and soon I was fast asleep.

I must have slept through the rest of the day and the whole of the night, for I awoke the next morning feeling utterly splendid! I was able to look back on the events of the past few days with a philosophical acceptance I found surprising in myself. I still believed Korzeniowski, Dutchke, Shaw and the rest totally misguided, but I could see that they were not inhuman monsters. They really believed they were working for the good of people they considered to be 'oppressed'.

I was feeling so rested I wondered if perhaps the food had been drugged, but when I turned my head I saw that Dutchke had evidently not slept as well. His eyes were red-rimmed and he was still in his outdoor clothes, his hands behind his head, staring moodily at the ceiling.

"You don't look too happy, Count von Dutchke," I said, getting up and moving towards the wash-basin.

"Why have any of us reason to be happy, Mr Bastable?" He uttered a sharp, bitter laugh. "I am cooped up here at a time when I should be out in the world, doing my work. I've no relish for Shaw's theatrical revolutionary posturings. A revolutionist should be silent, unseen, cautious . . ."

"You're not exactly unknown to the world," I pointed out, jumping a little as boiling hot water issued from the tap. "Your picture is frequently in the newspapers. Your books are widely distributed, I understand."

"That is not what I meant." He glared at me and then shut his eyes, as if to blot my presence from his mind.

I was faintly amused by the rivalries I had witnessed among the anarchists—or socialists or communards or whatever they chose to call themselves. Each seemed to have an individual dream of how the world should be ordered and resented all other versions of that dream. If they could only agree on certain essentials, I thought, they would be rather more effective.

I glanced out of the window as I dried my face. Not that Shaw had entirely failed. In the rose gardens I saw children of various ages and a variety of nationalities playing together, laughing joyfully as they ran about in the morning sunshine. And along the paths strolled men and women, chatting easily to each other and smiling frequently. Some were evidently married and not a few were members of the coloured races married to members of the white race. This did not shock me as it should have done. It all seemed natural to me. I remembered what Shaw had said the city was called —Democratic Dawn City—the City of Equality. But was such equality possible in the outside world? Was not Shaw's dream city artifically conceived? I expressed this thought to Dutchke, who had opened his eyes again, and added: "It *does* look tranquil—but isn't this place built on piracy and murder, just as you said London was built on injustice?"

He shrugged. "I don't much care to discuss Shaw's ambitions." Then he paused for a while. "But to be fair I think you could say that Dawn City is a beginning—

it is conceived in terms of the future. London is an ending—the final conception of a dead ideology."

"What do you mean?"

"Europe has used up its dream. It has no future. The future lies here, in China, which has a new dream, a new future. It lies in Africa, India—throughout the Middle East and the Far East—perhaps in South America, too. Europe is dying. I, for one, regret it. But before she dies, she offers certain notions of what is possible to the countries she has dishonoured . . ."

"You are saying we are decadent?"

"If you like. It is not what I said."

I could not completely follow his argument so I let it drop. I found my clothes, newly cleaned and pressed, at the end of my bed, and put them on.

A little later there was a tap at the door and an old, old man walked in. His hair was pure white and he had a long, white goatee beard after the Chinese fashion. He was dressed in simple cotton clothes and leaned on a stick. He looked as if he had lived a hundred years and seen a great deal of the world. When he spoke it was in a cracked, high-pitched voice with a thick accent I identified as Russian.

"Good morning, young man. Good morning, Dutchke."

Dutchke straightened up on the bed, his gloom forgotten, his face brightening.

"Uncle Vladimir! How are you?"

"I'm well, but feeling my age a little these days."

Dutchke introduced us as the old man sat down in one of the easy chairs. "Mr Bastable, this is Vladimir Ilyitch Ulianov. He was a revolutionist before any of us were born!"

I did not correct him on that point but shook hands with the old Russian.

Dutchke laughed. "Mr Bastable is a confirmed capitalist, uncle. He disapproves of us all—calls us anarchists and murderers!"

Ulianov chuckled without rancour. "It is always amusing to hear the mass-murderer accusing the man he seeks to destroy. I'll not forget the thousand accusations made against me in Russia in the twenties, before I had to leave. Kerensky was President then—is he still?"

"He died last year, uncle. They have elected a new President now. Prince Sukhanov is now leader of the Duma."

"And doubtless licks the spittle of the Romanovs as his predecessor did. Duma! A travesty of democracy. I was a fool even to let myself be elected to it. That is not the way to challenge injustice. The Tsar still rules Russia—even if it is nowadays through his so-called parliament."

"True, Vladimir Ilyitch," murmured Dutchke and I got the impression he was humouring the man a little. There was no doubting his admiration of this ancient revolutionist—but now he was tolerating him as one would a man who had done great things in his day but had now turned a trifle senile.

"Ah, if only I had had the opportunity," Ulianov went on, "I would have shown Kerensky what democracy really meant. We should have chained the Tsar's power —perhaps even kicked him out altogether. Yes—yes— it might have been possible, if all the people had risen up and opposed him. There must have been one moment in history when that could have happened, and I missed it. Perhaps I was sleeping, perhaps I was exiled in Germany at the time, perhaps I was" (he smiled fondly) "making love! Ha! But one day Russia *will* be free, eh, Rudolph? We shall make honest workers of the Romanovs and send Kerensky and his 'Parliament' to Siberia, just as they sent me there, eh? The revolution must come soon."

"Soon, uncle."

"Let the people starve a little longer. Let them be made to work a little harder. Let them know disease and fear and death a little better—then they will rise up. A tide of humanity which will sweep over the corrupt princes and merchants and drown them in their own blood!"

"As you say, uncle."

"Oh! If only I had had my chance. If I could have controlled the Duma—but that weasel Kerensky tricked me, discredited me, chased me from my own homeland, my Russia."

"You will return some day."

Ulianov winked cunningly at Dutchke. "I have returned once or twice already. I have distributed a few pamphlets. I have visited my rich politician friend Bronstein and given him a fright in case the Okharna should discover me at his house and think him a revolutionist, too. He *was* once, of course, but he chose to modify his views and keep his place in the Duma. Jews! They are all the same."

Dutchke looked a little disapproving at this sudden outburst. "There are Jews and Jews, uncle."

"True. But Bronstein—ah, what is the use—he is ninety-seven years old. Soon he will be dead and I will be dead."

"But your writings, Vladimir Ilyitch, will always live. They will inspire each new generation of revolutionists—all those who learn to hate injustice."

Ulianov nodded. "Yes," he said. "Let us hope so. But you will not remember . . ." And now he launched on a new series of repetitive anecdotes while Dutchke disguised his impatience and listened politely, even when the old man querulously attacked him, for a moment, as not following the True Way of the Revolution.

In the meantime I uttered the magic word 'Food' and the Chinese girl appeared in the milky-blue oval again. I asked for breakfast for three and it was duly delivered. Dutchke and I ate heartily, but Ulianov was loathe to waste time eating. He continued to drone on as we enjoyed our breakfast. Ulianov reminded me somewhat of the old Holy Men, the lamas I had occasionally come across in my former life as an officer in the Indian Army. Often his conversation seemed as abstract as did theirs. And yet, as I had respected those lamas, I respected Ulianov—for his age, for his Faith, for the way in which he would repeat the articles of his creed over and over again. He seemed a kindly, harmless old man—very different from my earlier image of a confirmed revolutionist.

The door opened as he launched into the phrase he had used earlier—"Let the people starve a little longer. Let them be made to work a little harder. Let them know disease and fear and death a little better—then they will rise up! A tide . . ." It was Shaw who stood in the doorway. He was dressed in a white linen suit and there was a panama hat on his head. He was smoking a cigar. "A tide of humanity which will sweep away injustice, eh, Vladimir Ilyitch?" He smiled. "But I disagree with you, as ever."

The old Russian looked up and wagged his finger. "You should not argue with one as old as me, Shuo Ho Ti. That is not the Chinese way. You should respect my words." He smiled back.

"What do you think, Mr Bastable?" Shaw asked banteringly. "Does despair breed revolution?"

"I know nothing of revolutions," I replied. "Though I might be induced to agree with you that a few reforms might be in order—in Russia, for instance."

Ulianov laughed. "A few reforms! Ho! That is what Kerensky wanted. But the reforms went by the board when it proved expedient to forget about them. It is always the same with 'reforms'. The *system* must die!"

"It is hope, Mr Bastable, not despair, which breeds revolution," said Shaw. "Give the people hope—show them what might be possible, what they can look forward to—then they might try to achieve something. Despair breeds only more despair—people lose heart and die in themselves. There is where Comrade Ulianov and those who follow him make a mistake. They think that people will rise up when their discomfort becomes unbearable. But that is not true. When their discomfort becomes totally unbearable—they *give* up. Offer them some extra comfort—and being human they will ask for more—and more—and more! Then comes revolution. Thus we of Dawn City work to distribute extra wealth among the coolies of China. We work to set an example in China which will encourage the oppressed peoples of the whole world."

Ulianov shook his head. "Bah! Bronstein had some such idea—but look what became of him!"

"Bronstein? Ah—your old enemy."

"He was once my friend," said Ulianov, suddenly sad. He got up with a sigh. "Still, we are all comrades here, even if we differ about methods." He gave me a long, hard look. "Do not think we are divided because we argue, Mr Bastable."

I had thought exactly that.

"We are human beings, you see," Ulianov continued. "We have fantastic dreams—but what the human mind can conceive, it can make reality. For good or ill. For good or ill."

"Perhaps for good *and* ill," I said.

"What do you mean?"

"Every coin has two sides. Every dream of perfection contains a nightmare of imperfection."

Ulianov smiled slowly. "That is perhaps why we should not aim for absolutes, eh? Is it absolutes which destroy themselves as surely as they destroy us?"

"Absolutes—and abstractions," I said. "There are little acts of justice as well as large ones, Vladimir Ilyitch Ulianov."

"You think that we revolutionists forsake our humanity to follow fantasies of utopia?"

"Perhaps not you . . ."

"You have voiced the eternal problem of the dedicated follower of any faith, Mr Bastable. There is never a resolution."

"Judging by my own experience," I said, "there is never a resolution to any problem concerning human affairs. I suppose you could call *that* philosophy 'British pragmatism'. Take it as it comes. . . ."

"The British certainly took it," said Dutchke and laughed. "There is a particular joy, I am sure you will agree, in looking for alternatives and seeing whether those alternatives will work and if they are better."

"There must be a better alternative to this world," said Ulianov feelingly. "There must be!"

Shaw had come to take us on a tour of his city. The four of us—Captain Korzeniowski, now fully recovered and with not even a scar to show for his headwound, Una Persson, Count von Dutchke and myself—followed Shaw from the apartment house and down a wide, sunlit street.

Dawn City continued to be an education for me, who had always seen revolutionists in terms of simpleminded nihilists, blowing up buildings, murdering people, with no idea of what they might want to build on the ruins of the world they were destroying. And here was their dream made reality.

But wasn't it a slightly spurious reality? I wondered. Could it actually be extended throughout the world?

When I had first been hurled into the world of the 1970s I had thought I had found Utopia. And now I was discovering that it was only a Utopia for some. Shaw wanted a Utopia which would exist for all.

I remembered the blood I had seen spread across the bridge of *The Rover*. Barry's blood. It was hard to reconcile that image with the one before me now.

Shaw took us to see schools, communal restaurants, workshops, laboratories, theatres, studios, all full of happy, relaxed people of a hundred different nationalities, races and creeds. I was impressed.

"This is what the whole of the East—and Africa—might have been like by now if it had not been for the European's greed," Shaw told me. "By now we would be economically stronger than Europe. That would be a true balance of power. Then you would see what justice was all about!"

"But it is a European ideal that you follow," I pointed out. "If we had not brought it . . ."

"We should have found it. People learn by example,

Mr Bastable. They do not have to have ideas forced upon them."

We had entered a darkened hall. Before us was a large kinema screen. Shaw bade us be seated and then the screen flickered into life.

I watched in horrified fascination as I saw pictures of Chinese men and women being decapitated in their scores.

"The village of Shihnan in Japanese Manchuria," said Shaw in a hard, flat voice. "The villagers failed to produce their annual quota of rice and are being punished. This happened last year."

I saw Japanese soldiers laughing as their long swords rose and fell.

I was stunned. "But that is Japan. . . ." was all I could say.

A new series of pictures. Coolies working on a railway line. Uniformed men were using whips to force them to work harder. The uniforms were Russian.

"Everyone knows the Russians are cruel in their treatment of subject peoples. . . ."

Shaw made no comment.

A rabble of Chinese—many of them women and children—armed with farm implements were rushing towards a stone wall. The people were in rags and half-starved. Gunfire broke out from behind the wall and the people fell down, twisted, bleeding, shrieking in agony. I could hardly bear to look. The gunfire continued until all the people were dead.

Men in brown uniforms with wide-brimmed hats appeared from behind the wall and moved amongst the corpses, checking that none lived.

"Americans!"

"To be fair," General Shaw said tonelessly, "they were acting at the request of the Siam government. That scene took place a few miles from Bangkok. American troops are helping the government to keep order. There have been a number of minor rebellions in some parts of Siam recently."

The next scene was an Indian township. Concrete huts were arranged in neat rows for as far as the eye could see.

"It's deserted," I said.

"Wait."

The camera took us along the desolate streets until we were outside the township. Here were soldiers in British red. They were wielding spades, heaping bodies into trenches filled with lime.

"Cholera?"

"There was cholera—typhoid—malaria—smallpox—but that was not why the whole village died. Look."

The camera moved in closer and I saw that there were many bullet wounds in the bodies.

"They marched on Delhi without passes to enter the city limits," said Shaw. "They refused to halt when ordered to do so. They were all shot down."

"But it could not have been an official decision," I said. "An officer panicked. It sometimes happens."

"Were the Russians, the Japanese, the Americans panicking?"

"No."

"This is how your kind of power is used when others threaten it," said Shaw. I looked at his eyes. There were tears in them.

I knew something of what he was feeling. There were tears in my eyes, too.

I tried to tell myself that the films were counterfeit —played by actors to impress people like me. But I knew that they were not counterfeit.

I left the kinema. I was shaking. I felt sick. And I was still weeping.

We walked in silence through the tranquil City of the Dawn, none of us able to speak after what we had witnessed. We came to the edge of the settlement and looked out over the makeshift airpark. There were men there now, working on the girders for what was evidently to be a good-sized mooring mast. We saw *The Rover* still pegged to the ground in her spider-web of cables, but the bigger ship had gone.

"Where is the *Loch Etive?*" It was Korzeniowski who spoke.

Shaw looked up absently and then, as if remembering a duty, smiled. "Oh, she is on her way back. I hope her second mission will be as successful as her first."

"Missions?" said Dutchke. "What missions?"

"Her first was to shoot down the Imperial Japanese Airship *Kanazawa*. We have armed her with some experimental guns. They are excellent. No recoil at all. Always the problem with big guns aboard an airship, eh?"

"True," said Korzeniowski. He took out his pipe and began to light it. "True."

"And her second mission was to bomb a section of the Trans-Siberian railroad and steal the cargo of a certain Moscow-bound train. I recently heard that the cargo was stolen. If it is what I hope, we shall be able to speed up Project NFB."

"Just what *is* this mysterious project?" Una Persson asked.

General O. T. Shaw gestured towards a large building like a factory which stood on the far side of the airpark. "Over there. A very expensive project, I don't mind saying. But I can't tell you any more, I'm afraid. I hardly understand it myself. Most of our German and Hungarian exiles are working on it. There are one or two Americans, too, and an Englishman—all political refugees. But brilliant and original scientists. Dawn City benefits by the tyranny imposed on curiosity in the West."

I could not believe that he had not considered the consequences of these actions. "You have now earned the wrath of three great powers," I said. "You stole a British airship to destroy a Japanese man-o'-war and a Russian railway. They are bound to get together. Dawn City will be lucky if it lasts a day!"

"We still have the hostages from the *Loch Etive*," Shaw murmured serenely.

"Will that knowledge stop the Japanese or the Russians from bombing you to bits?"

"It offers a serious diplomatic problem. The three nations must argue it over for a while. In the meantime we are finishing off our defences."

"Even you can't defend yourself against the combined aerial fleets of Britain, Japan and Russia!" I said.

"We shall have to see," said Shaw. "Now, Mr Bastable, what did you think of my magic lantern show?"

"You convinced me that a closer watch should be kept on how the natives are treated," I said.

"And that is all?"

"There *are* other ways of stopping injustice," I said, "than revolution and bloody war."

"Not if the cancer is to be burned out completely," said Korzeniowski. "I realise that now."

"Aha," said Shaw, looking towards the hills. "Here comes the *Fei-chi*...."

"The what?"

"The flying machine."

"I can't see it," said Korzeniowski.

I, too, could see no sign of the *Loch Etive*, though I heard a drone like that of a mosquito.

"Look," said Shaw grinning, "there!"

A speck appeared on the horizon and the droning became a shrill whine.

"There!" He giggled in excitement. "I don't mean an airship—I mean the *Fei-chi*—the little hornet—here she comes!"

Instinctively I ducked as something whizzed over my head. I looked up. I had an impression of several windmill sails spinning at fantastic speed, of long, bird-like wings, and then it was disappearing in the distance, still voicing the same angry whine.

"My God!" said Korzeniowski, removing the pipe from his mouth and registering his amazement for the first time since I had met him. "It's a heavier than air flying machine. I was sure—I was always told—such a thing was impossible."

Shaw grinned, almost breaking into a dance in his delight. "And I have fifty of them, captain! Fifty little hornets with very bad stings. Now you see why I feel up to defending Dawn City against anything the Great Powers send!"

"They seem a bit fragile to me," I said.

"They are a bit," Shaw admitted, "but they can travel at speeds of nearly five hundred miles an hour. And that is their strength. Who would have time to train a gun on one of those before a *Fei-chi* had been able to burst the hull of a flying ironclad with its special explosive bullets?"

"Who—how did you come by this invention?" Dutchke wanted to know.

"Oh, one of my American outlaws had the idea," Shaw returned airily. "And some of my French engineers made it practicable. We built and flew the first machine in less than a week. Within a month we had developed it into what you have just seen."

"I admire the man who would go up in one of those," said Dutchke. "Aren't they crushed by such speeds?"

"They have to wear special padded clothing, certainly. And, of course, their reactions must be as fast as their machines if they are to control them properly."

Korzeniowski shook his head. "Well," he said, "I think I'll stick to airships. They're altogether more credible than those contraptions. I've seen it—but I still can't believe in heavier than air machines."

Shaw looked almost cunningly at me. "Well, Mr Bastable? Are you still convinced I am mad?"

I continued to stare into the sky where the *Fei-chi* had disappeared. "You are not mad in the way I first thought," I admitted. A sense of terrible foreboding seized me. I wished with all my heart that I was back in my own time where heavier than air flying machines and wireless telephones and coloured, talking kinemas which came to life in one's room were the fantasies of children and lunatics. I thought of Mr H. G. Wells and I turned, looking towards the building which housed Project NFB. "I suppose you haven't invented a Time Machine, by any chance?"

The Warlord grinned. "Not yet, Mr. Bastable. But we are thinking about it. Why do you ask?"

I shook my head and did not reply.

Dutchke clapped me on the back. "You want to know where all this leads, don't you? You want to travel into the future and see General Shaw's Utopia!" He had been quite won over to Shaw's side now.

I shrugged. "I think I've had my fill of Utopias," I murmured.


CHAPTER V

The Coming of the Air Fleets


THROUGHOUT THE DAYS which followed I made no attempt to escape Dawn City. The whole idea would have been pointless anyway. General O. T. Shaw's men controlled all roads and guarded both the airships and the sheds where the new *Fei-chi* 'hornets' were stored. Sometimes I would watch as the *Fei-chi* were tested by their tall, Chinese pilots—healthy, confident young men completely dedicated to Shaw's cause, able to accept the heavier than air machines as I could not.

Early on I assured myself that the *Loch Etive* hostages were safe and well and I chatted with one or two fellows I had known on board her, learning that Captian Harding had indeed died not long after being sent home to that little house in Balham where he had lodged during his leaves. Another acquaintance had died, too. In an out-of-date newspaper I read that Cornelius Dempsey had been shot in a street battle with armed policemen. Dempsey had been part of a gang of anarchists trapped in a house in East London. So far his body had not been found, but several witnesses confirmed that he had been dead when his friends carried him away. I felt sadness overwhelming me and adding to that mood of bitterness and depression which had come while I watched those terrible kinema films.

More recent newspapers brought in by Shaw's men were full of reports of Shuo Ho Ti's daring raids, his acts of piracy and murder. One or two of the papers saw him as 'the first modern bandit' and it was they, I think, who dubbed him 'Warlord of the Air'. Certainly, while England strove to halt Russian and Japanese military airships from taking instant vengeance and the Chinese Central Government vainly attempted to stop any aerial warships entering their territory, Shaw pulled off a series of amazing raids, descending from the sky on trains, motor convoys, ships and military and scientific establishments to get what he needed. What he did not need he distributed to the Chinese population —his repainted 'flagship', now no longer the *Loch Etive* but the *Shan-tien* (Lightning) and flying his familiar crimson flags, appearing in the skies over an impoverished village or town and showering money, goods and food—as well as pamphlets telling the people to join Shuo Ho Ti, the Peacemaker, in the freeing of China from foreign oppression. Thousands came to swell the ranks of his army at the far end of the Valley of the Morning. And Shaw added more ships to his fleet, bringing merchant vessels to land at gunpoint, releasing crews and passengers, flying the captured craft back to Dawn City and there refitting them with his new cannon. The only problem was a shortage among his own followers of men trained to fly the craft. Inexperienced commanders had put their ships into danger more than once and two had been lost through incompetence. A couple of times Shaw proposed that I should become his ally and help fly a ship of my choice, but I refused, for the only reason I would board an airship would be to escape and I did not wish to indulge in piracy just so that I might find a chance of gaining my freedom.

Nonetheless there were conversations with the Warlord in which he described his past to me as he continued to try to win me over.

His was an interesting story. He had been the son of an English missionary and his Chinese wife who had worked in a remote Shantung village for years until they came to the attention of the old Warlord—'a *traditional* bandit' Shaw called him—of their part of the world. The Warlord, Lao-Shu, had killed his father and taken his mother as a concubine. He had been brought up as one of Lao-Shu's many children and eventually ran away to Peking where his father's brother taught. He had been sent to school in England where he had been very unhappy and learned to hate what he considered the English superiority towards other races, classes and creeds. Later he went to Oxford where he did well and began to 'realise', as he put it, that imperialism was a disease which robbed the majority of the world's population of its dignity and the right to order its own affairs. These were English conceptions, he was the first to admit, but what he resented was that they were reserved for the English alone. "The conqueror always assumes that his moral superiority—rather than his ferocious greed—is what has allowed him to triumph." Leaving Oxford, he had entered the army and done well, learning all he could of English military matters, then getting transferred to the Crown Colony of Hong Kong to serve in the police—for, of course, he spoke fluent Mandarin and Cantonese. He had soon deserted the police, taking with him his whole detachment of native soldiers, two steamcarts and a considerable amount of artillery. Then he had gone back to Shantung where the Warlord still ruled and—

"There I killed my father's murderer and took his place," he said baldly.

His mother had died in the meantime. With his connections with revolutionists throughout the world he had conceived the idea of Dawn City. He would take from Europe what, in its pride, it rejected—its brilliant scientists, engineers, politicians and writers who were too clever to be tolerated by their own governments—and he would use it to the benefit of his China.

"It is part of what Europe owes us," he pointed out. "And soon we shall be able to claim the rest of the debt. Do you know how they first began the ruin of China, Mr Bastable? It was the English, mainly, but also the Americans. They grew opium in India—vast fields of it—and secretly shipped it into China where, officially, it was banned. This created such inflation (for those who smuggled it in were paid in Chinese silver) that the whole economy was ruined. When the Chinese government objected to this, the foreigners sent in armies to teach the Chinese a lesson for their arrogance in complaining. Those armies found a country in economic ruin and huge sections of the population smoking opium. Naturally, the only thing which could have brought this about was an innate decadence, a moral inferiority. . . ." Shaw laughed. "The opium clippers were specially designed for the China trade, to run swiftly from India with their cargoes, and often they carried Bibles as well as opium, for the missionaries would insist that if they, who could speak pidgin Chinese, were to translate for the smugglers, they must be allowed to distribute Bibles as well. After that, there was no looking back. And Europeans think Chinese hatred of them unreasonable!"

Shaw would become serious at times like these and would say to me: "Foreign devils? You think 'devils' is a strong enough word, Mr Bastable?"

Now his ambitions extended to the taking back of the whole of China:

"And soon the great grey factories of Shanghai will be ours. The laboratories and schools and museums of Peking will be ours. The trading and manufacturing centres of Canton will be ours. The rich rice fields—

all will be ours!" His eyes gleamed. "China will be united. The foreigners will be driven out and all will be equal. We shall set an example to the world."

"If you are successful," I said quietly, "let the world also see that you are human. People are impressed by kindness as well as by factories and military strength."

Shaw gave me a peculiar stare.

There were now some fifteen airships tied up to the mooring masts on the field beyond Dawn City and there were nearly a hundred *Fei-chi* in the hangars. The whole valley was defended with artillery and infantry and could withstand an attack from any quarter when it came; and we knew it would come.

We? I don't know how I had come to identify myself with bandits and revolutionists—and yet there was no mistaking the fact that I had. I refused to join them, but I hoped that they might win. Win against the ships of my own nation which would come against them and which, doubtless, would be destroyed by them. How I had changed in the past couple of weeks! I could contemplate, without horror, the bloody deaths of British servicemen. Comrades.

But I had to face the fact that the people of Dawn City were my comrades now—even though I would not commit myself to their cause. I did not want Dawn City and all it represented to be destroyed. I wanted General O. T. Shaw—the Warlord of the Air—to drive the foreigners from his nation and make it strong again.

I waited in trepidation for the 'enemy'—my countrymen—to come.

I was lying in my bed asleep when the news came through on the *tien-ying* ('electric shadow') machine. The milky-blue oval became General Shaw's face. He looked grim and he looked excited.

"They are on their way, Mr Bastable. I thought you might like to be awake for the show."

"Who . . ." I murmured blearily. "What . . . ?"

"The air fleets—American, British, Russian, Japanese and some French, I believe—they are coming to the Valley of the Morning—coming to punish John Chinaman. . . ."

I saw his head move and he spoke more rapidly.

"I must go now. Shall we see you at the ringside—the main headquarters building?"

"I'll be there." As the picture faded I sprang out of bed and washed and dressed; then hurried through the quiet streets of Dawn City until I reached the circular tower which was the city's chief administrative building. There was, of course, furious activity. A wireless telephone message had been received from the British flagship *Victoria Imperatrix* saying that if the *Loch Etive* hostages were freed Shaw might send out with them his people's women and children who would not be harmed. Shaw replied bluntly. The hostages were already being taken to the far end of the valley where they would be released. The people of Dawn City would fight together and, if necessary, die together. The *Victoria Imperatrix* offered the information that there were a hundred airships on their way to Dawn City and that therefore Dawn City could not possibly hope to last more than an hour against such a fleet. Shaw replied that he felt Dawn City might last a little longer and he looked forward to the arrival of the battle-fleet. In the meantime, he said, he had recently received the interesting news that two Japanese flying gunboats had devasted a village which had received help from Shaw. The British, doubtless, would be making similar reprisals? At this, H.M.A.S. *Victoria Imperatrix* cut off communication with Dawn City. Shaw smiled bleakly.

He saw me standing in the room. "Hello, Bastable. By God! The Japanese have got a lot to answer for where China's concerned. I'd like to . . . What's this?" An assistant handed him a sheet of paper. "Good. Good. Project NFB is proceeding apace."

"Where is Captain Korzeniowski?" I saw Count Rudolph and Una Persson on the other side of the room talking to one of Shaw's cotton-clad 'majors', but I could not see Mrs Persson's father.

"Korzeniowski is back in command of *The Rover*," said Shaw, pointing towards the airpark, plainly visible from this tower. I saw tiny figures running back and forth as their ships prepared to take the air. So far there was no sign of the *Fei-chi* flying machines. "And look," added Shaw, "here comes the battle-fleet."

I thought at first that I saw a massive bank of black cloud moving over the horizon of the hills and blotting out the pale sunshine. With the cloud came a great thrumming sound, like many deep-voiced gongs being beaten rapidly in unison. The sound grew louder as the cloud began to fill the whole sky, casting a dark and ominous shadow over the Valley of the Morning.

It was the allied Air Fleet of five nations.

Each ship was a thousand feet long. Each had a hull as strong as steel. Each bristled with artillery and great grenades which could be dropped upon their enemies. Each ship moved implacably through the sky, keeping pace with its mighty fellows. Each was dedicated to exacting fierce vengeance upon the upstarts who had sought to question the power of those it served. A shoal of monstrous flying sharks, confident that they controlled the skies and, from the skies, the land.

Ships of Japan, with the Imperial crimson sun emblazoned on their white and gleaming hulls.

Ships of Russia, with great black double-headed eagles glaring from hulls of deepest scarlet, claws spread as if to strike.

Ships of France, on which the tricoleur flag spread on the backgrounds of blue was a piece of blatant hypocrisy; a sham of republicanism and an affront to the ideals of the French Revolution.

Ships of America, bearing the Stars and Stripes, no longer the banner of Liberty.

Ships of Britain.

Ships with cannon and bombs and crews who, in

their pride, thought it was to be a simple matter to raze Dawn City and what it stood for.

Shark-ships, rapacious and cruel and arrogant, their booming engines like triumphant anticipatory laughter. Could we withstand them, even for an instant? I doubted it.

Now our ground defences had opened up. Shells sped into the sky and exploded around the ships of the mighty Air Fleet, but on they came, through the smoke and flame, careless and haughty, closer and closer to Dawn City itself. And now our own tiny fleet began to rise from the airpark to meet the invaders—fifteen modified merchantmen against a hundred specially designed men-o'-war. They had the advantange of the recoilless guns and could 'stand' in the air and shoot much longer and more accurately than the larger vessels, but there were few weak points on those flying ironclads and most of the explosive shells at worst only blackened the paint of the hulls or cracked the windows in the gondolas.

There was a bellow and fire sprouted from the leading British airship, H.M.A.S. *Edwardus Rex*, as its guns answered ours. I saw the hull of one of our ships crumple and the whole vessel plunge towards the rocky ground of the foothills, little figures leaping overboard in the hope of somehow escaping the worst of the impact. Black smoke curled everywhere over the scene. There came an explosion and a blaze of flame as our ship struck the ground and its engines blew up, the fuel oil igniting instantly.

Shaw was staring grimly through the window, controlling the formation of our ships through a wireless telephone. How hard it had been to make an impact on the enemy fleet—and how easily they had destroyed our ship!

*Boom! Boom!*

Again the great guns roared. Again an adapted merchantman buckled in the air and sank to the earth.

Only now did I wish that I had accepted a commission on one of the ships. Only now did I feel the urge to join the fight, to retaliate, as much as anything, out of a spirit of fair play.

*Boom!*

It was *The Rover*, spiralling down with two engines on fire and its hull buckling in half as the helium rushed into the atmosphere. I watched tensely as it fell, praying there would be enough gas left in the hull to let the ship come down relatively lightly. But that was a hundred tons of metal and plastic and guns and men falling through the sky. I closed my eyes and winced as I thought I felt the tremor of its impact with the ground.

I was in no doubt of Korzeniowski's fate.

But then, as if inspired by the old captain's heroic death, the *Shan-tien* (the old *Loch Etive*) offered a broadside to the Japanese flagship, the *Yokomoto,* and must have struck right through to her ammunition store for she exploded in a thousand fiery fragments and there was scarcely a recogniseable scrap of her left when the explosion had died.

Now we saw two more ships go down—an American and a French—and we cheered. We all cheered save for Una Persson who was looking bleakly out at the spot where *The Rover* had disappeared. Dutchke was in animated conversation with the major and did not seem to notice his mistress's grief. I went over to her and touched her shoulder.

"Perhaps he is only wounded," I said.

She smiled at me through her tears and shook her head. "He is dead," she said. "He died bravely, didn't he?"

"As he lived," I said.

She seemed puzzled. "I thought you hated him."

"I thought I did. But I loved him."

She pulled herself together at this and nodded, putting out a slender hand and letting the tips of the fingers rest for a moment on my sleeve. "Thank you, Mr Bastable. I hope my father has not died for nothing."

"We are giving a good account of ourselves," I said.

But I saw that we had at most five ships left from the original fifteen and there were still nearly ninety allied battleships in the sky.

Shaw looked up, listening carefully. "Infantry and motorised cavalry attacking the valley on all sides," he said. "Our men are standing firm." He listened a little longer. "I don't think we've much to fear from that quarter at the moment."

The invading ships had not yet reached Dawn City. They had been forced to defend themselves against our first aerial attack and, now that our gunners were getting their range from the ground, one or two more were hit.

"Time to send up the *Fei-chi*, I think." Shaw telephoned the order. "The Great Powers think they have won! Now we shall show them our real strength!" He telephoned the soldiers defending the building housing Project NFB and reminded them that on no account should a ship be allowed to attack the place. The mysterious project was evidently of paramount importance in his strategy.

I could not see the hangars where the 'hornets' were stored and my first glimpse of the winged and whirling little flying machines was when they climbed through the black smoke and began to spray the hulls of the flying ironclads with explosive bullets, attacking from above and diving down on their opponents who, doubtless, were still hardly aware of what was happening.

The *Victoria Imperatrix* went down. The *Theodore Roosevelt* went down. The *Alexandre Nevsky* went down. The *Tashiyawa* went down. The *Emperor Napoleon* and the *Pyat* went down. One after another they fell from the air, circling slowly or breaking up rapidly, but falling; without a doubt they were falling. And it did not seem that a single delicate *Fei-chi*, flown by only two men—an aviator and a gunner—had been hit. The guns of the foreign ships were simply not designed to hit such tiny targets. They roared and belched their huge shells in all directions, but they were baffled, like clumsy sea-cows attacked by sharp-toothed piranha fish, they simply did not know how to defend themselves. The Valley of the Morning was littered with their wreckage. A thousand fires burned in the hills, showing where the proud aerial ironclads had met their end. Half the allied fleet had been destroyed and five of our airships (including the *Shan-tien*) were now coming in to moor, leaving the fighting to the *Fei-chi*. Evidently the shock of facing the tiny heavier than air machines was too much for the attackers. They had seen their finest ships blown from the skies in a matter of minutes. Slowly the cumbersome men-o'-war turned and began to retreat. Not a single bomb had fallen on Dawn City.

# CHAPTER VI

### Another Meeting with the Amateur Archaeologist

WE HAD, AT some cost, won the first engagement, but there were many more still to come before we should know if we had driven the Great Powers away for good. We learned that their land invasion had also met with failure and that the allied forces had withdrawn. We exulted.

During the next few days we waited and recouped our strength and it was during this period that I, at last, offered my services to the Warlord of the Air who accepted without comment of any kind and put me in command of my old ship, now the *Shan-tien*.

It was confirmed that Captain Korzeniowski and his entire crew had been killed when *The Rover* was shot down.

Then the attack began afresh and I prepared to go aboard my ship, but Shaw asked me to remain in the headquarters tower for it had become swiftly evident that the ships of the Great Powers had adopted a more cautious strategy. They came as far as the hills on the horizon and hovered there while they tried to shell the sheds where our *Fei-chi* were stored. I noticed, once again, that Shaw seemed more anxious for the safety of the Project NFB building than for the flying machine sheds, but neither were badly hit, as it turned out.

I felt an appalling sense of outrage, however, when some of the shells exploded in Dawn City, damaging the pretty houses, breaking windows, blasting trees and flower-beds, and I waited impatiently for orders to go to my ship. But Shaw remained cool and he let the enemy expend his fire-power for nearly an hour before he ordered the *Fei-chi* into the sky.

"But what about me?" I said, aggrieved. "Aren't you going to let me have a crack at them? I've several deaths to avenge, you know—not least Korzeniowski's."

"We all have much to avenge, Captain Bastable." (As was his practice he had conferred a high-sounding rank on me). "And it is not quite the time, I'm afraid, to let you take yours. The *Shan-tien* is to fly the most important assignment of them all. But not yet—not yet. . . ."

That was all I could get from him then.

Once again our heavier than air machines drove the flying ironclads beyond the hills and destroyed seven in the process. But this time we had casualties, for the airships had equipped themselves with fast-firing machine guns which could be mounted on the tops of the hulls in hastily manufactured armoured turrets where they could, while they lasted, give good retaliatory fire. The delicate two-man machines were easily destroyed once hit and we lost six during that second engagement.

The attack continued for nearly two weeks with constant reinforcements being brought up by the enemy, but with our own reserves slowly dwindling. I don't think even Shaw had expected the Great Powers to show such absolute resolve to destroy him. It was as if they felt their grip on all their territories would weaken if they were beaten by the Warlord. We heard encouraging news, however. All over China peasants and workers and students were turning on their oppressors. The entire nation was in the grip of revolution. Shaw's hope was that trouble would break out in so many areas at once that the allied forces would be spread too thinly to be effective.

As it was, Dawn City had forced the Powers to concentrate much of their strength in one area and successful revolts had taken place in Shanghai (now in the control of a revolutionary committee) and Peking (where the occupying Japanese had been bloodily put to death) as well as other cities and parts of provinces.

From Dawn City Shaw heard the news of his revolution's spreading and his spirits rose, even as our supplies shrank.

Yet still we managed to hold the combined strength of the Great Powers at bay and Shaw took an even keener interest in the progress of that secret project of his.

One morning I was walking from my sleeping quarters to the central tower when I heard a commotion ahead of me and broke into a run. I found a crowd of people staring out at the airpark and pointing into the sky.

In astonishment I saw that a single airship was drifting in, its engines dead. There was no mistaking the Union Jack emblazoned on its tailplanes. Hurriedly I ran towards the headquarters tower, certain that they must have seen the mysterious ship by now.

As I reached the door of the tower there came an enormous explosion which made the whole place shudder. I entered the lift and was borne swiftly up to the top of the building.

The little British airship—not nearly so large as the men-o'-war we had learned to expect—was bombing the *Fei-chi* sheds! It had waited for a favourable wind and then drifted in at night, unseen and unheard, with the object of destroying our flying machines.

Already every gun we had was opening up on the airship, which was very low in the sky. Luckily its bombs had not yet struck the sheds themselves, though several smoking craters showed that it had only just missed. This was no heavily armoured ship and its hull soon burst, the ship plummeting down stern first and bouncing right across the airpark, narrowly missing our tethered 'fleet' before coming to a stop. Immediately I and a number of others left the tower and climbed into a motor car. We raced out of Dawn City and across the airpark to where the ship was already being surrounded by Shaw's colourfully dressed bandit-soldiers. As I thought, few of the crew had been badly hurt. For the first time on that shattered hull I saw the name of the ship and I received a shock of recognition. I had almost forgotten it. It was the first airship I had ever seen. Evidently the British had called upon their Indian airfleet to give assistance. The survey ship I saw broken on the ground, quite close to the Project NFB building, was none other than the *Pericles*—the ship which had saved my life.

It gave me an odd turn to see that ship again, I don't mind admitting. I realised that the Great Powers must be using every ship they could spare in their efforts to destroy Dawn City.

And then I saw Major Powell himself come staggering from the wreckage, a wild look in his dark eyes. His face was smeared with oil and his uniform was torn. One arm was limp at his side, but he still clutched his baton as he supervised his men's escape from the ship. He recognised me right away.

His voice was high and strained. "Hello, Bastable. In league with our Coloured Brethren now, are you? Well, well—wasn't much good saving your life, was it?"

"Good morning, major," I said. "Let me compliment you on your bravery."

"Stupidity. Still, it was worth a try. You can't win, you know—for all your bloody little airboats. We'll get you in the end."

"It's costing you rather a lot, though," I pointed out.

Powell glared around suspiciously at Shaw's soldiers. "What are they going to do? Torture us to death? Send our bodies back as a warning to others?"

"You'll be well treated," I told him. I fell into step with him as he and his men were disarmed and escorted back towards Dawn City. "I'm sorry about the *Pericles*."

"So am I." He was almost crying—whether with fury or with sorrow, I could not tell. "So that's what you were —a bloody nihilist. That's why you claimed to have amnesia. And to think I believed you were one of us."

"I was one of you," I said quietly. "Maybe I still am. I don't know."

"This is a bad show, Bastable. All China in revolt. Parts of India have caught the fever now, not to mention what's going on in South East Asia. Poor benighted natives think they've got a chance. They haven't, of course."

"I think they have—now," I said. "The days of imperialism are ending—at least, as we understand it."

"If they are ending—it's to plunge us all back into the Dark Ages. The Great Powers have ensured the peace of the world for a hundred years—and now it's all over. It'll take a decade to get back to normal, if we ever do."

"It will never be 'normal' again," I said. "That peace, major, was bought at too dear a price."

He grunted. "They've certainly converted you. But they'll never convert me. You'd rather have war in Europe, would you?"

"A war in Europe should have happened a long time

ago. A war between the Great Powers would have destroyed their grip on their subject peoples. Don't you see that?"

"I don't see anything of the kind. I feel like someone witnessing the last days of the Roman Empire. Damn!" He winced as he struck his arm against a shed.

"I'll get that arm attended to as soon as we reach the city," I said.

"Don't want your charity," said Powell. "Bloody Chinks and niggers running the world—that's a laugh."

I left him then and I did not see him again.

If I had been in two minds about my loyalties before, I was no longer. Powell's parting sneer of contempt had succeeded in my deciding to choose Shaw's side once and for all. The mask of kindly patronage had dropped away to show the hatred and the fear beneath.

When I got back to the central tower Shaw was waiting for me. He looked resolute.

"That sneak attack determined something," he said. "Project NFB is complete. I think it will be successful, though there is no time—or method—to test it. We shall do what that ship did. We'll leave tonight."

"I think you had better explain a little more clearly," I smiled. "What are we to do?"

"The Great Powers are using the big airship yards at Hiroshima as their main base. That is where they go for repairs and spares. It is the only relatively nearby place where they can be serviced properly. Also it is where many of the big flying ironclads are built. If we destroy that base—we have considerably greater flexibility of manoeuvre, Captain Bastable."

"I agree," I said. "But we haven't enough airships to do it, General Shaw. We have very few bombs. The *Fei-chi* cannot fly that distance. Also there is every likelihood that we shall be sighted and shot down when we leave the Valley of the Morning or at any point beyond it. How can we possibly do it?"

"Project NFB is ready. Is there a chance of taking the

*Shan-tien* out tonight and getting past the allied ships?"

"We've as good a chance as that ship had in reaching here," I said. "If the wind's right."

"Then be ready to leave, Captain Bastable, at sunset."

I shrugged. It was suicide. But I would do it.

## CHAPTER VII

### Project NFB

BY SUNSET WE were all aboard. During the day there had been a few desultory attacks by the enemy airships, but no serious damage had been done.

"They are waiting for reinforcements," Shaw told me. "And those reinforcements, according to my information, are due to come from Hiroshima, starting out tomorrow morning."

"It's going to be a long flight for us," I said. "We'll not be back by morning, even if we're successful."

"Then we'll go to Peking. It is in the hands of fellow revolutionists now."

"True."

Ulianov, Dutchke and Una Persson had come aboard with General Shaw. "I want them to see it so that they will believe it," he told me. Also on board were a number of scientists who had supervised the loading of a fairly large object into our lower hold. These were serious looking Hungarians, Germans and Americans and they said nothing to me. But they had an Australian with them and I asked him what was going on.

He grinned. "Going *up*, you mean. Ha ha! Somebody ought to tell you, but it's not my job. Good luck, sport."

And he left with the rest of his fellow scientists.

General Shaw put an arm round my shoulders. "Don't worry, Bastable. You'll know before we get there."

"It must be a bomb," I said. "A particularly powerful bomb? Nitro-glycerine? A fire bomb?"

"Wait."

We all stood on the bridge of the *Loch Etive* watching the sun go down. The ship—I should call her the *Shan-tien*—was not the luxury liner I had known. She had been stripped of every non-essential fitting and through her portholes jutted the snouts of General O. T. Shaw's recoilless guns. What had been promenade decks were now artillery platforms. Where passengers had danced, ammunition was stored. If we were discovered, we should give a good account of ourselves. I thought back to that stupid incident with 'Roughrider Ronnie' Reagan. But for him, I should not today be in command of this ship, flying a foolhardy assignment whose nature I could not even guess at. It seemed that more time had passed since my encounter with Reagan than had passed since I had been flung from my own time into the future.

Ulianov came up beside me as I stood at my controls and began to prepare to let slip from the mast.

"Brooding, young man?"

I looked into his old, kindly eyes. "I was wondering what made a decent English army officer turn into a desperate revolutionist overnight," I smiled.

"It happens to many like that," he said. "I have seen them. But you have to show them so *much* injustice first. . . . Nobody wants to believe that the world is cruel—or that one's own kind are cruel. Not to know cruelty is to remain innocent, eh? And we should all like to remain innocent. A revolutionist is a man who, perhaps, fails to keep his innocence but so desperately wants it back that he seeks to create a world where all shall be innocent in that way."

"But can such a world ever exist, Vladimir Ilyitch?" I sighed. "You're describing the Garden of Eden, you know. A familiar dream—but a reality? I wonder. . . ."

"There are an infinite number of possible societies. In an infinite universe, all may become real sooner or later. Yet it is always up to mankind to make real what it really wishes to be real. Man is a creature capable of building almost anything he pleases—or destroying anything he pleases. Sometimes, as old as I am, I am astonished by him!" He chuckled.

I smiled back, reflecting that he would be really astonished if he knew that, in effect, I was older than him!

It became dark and I drew a deep breath. Our only light came from the illuminated instrument panels. I intended to get the ship up to three thousand feet and remain at that height for as long as possible. The wind was blowing in roughly a North Easterly direction and would take us the way we needed to go if we were to leave the valley without recourse to our engines.

"Let slip," I said.

Our mooring lines fell away and we began to rise. I heard the wind whistling about our hull. I saw the lights of Dawn City dropping down below us.

"Three thousand feet, Height Coxswain." I said. "Take it slowly. Forty-five degrees elevation. Turn her portside on to the wind, Steering Cox." I checked our compass. "Keep her steady."

Everyone was silent. Dutchke and Una Persson stood at the window, staring down. Shaw and Ulianov stood near me, peering at instruments which meant next to nothing to them. Shaw was dressed in a blue cotton suit and was puffing on a cigarette. On his head was tilted a coolie hat of woven reeds. There was a holstered revolver at his belt. After a while he began to pace back and forth across the bridge.

We were drifting slowly over the hills. Within minutes we should be over the main enemy camp and in range of their artillery. If we were sighted they could swiftly send up several ships and there would be little doubt of the outcome. We should be blown from the sky, along with Project NFB. With Shaw dead, I doubted if Dawn City would have the will to carry on the fight much longer.

But at last the camp was behind us and we relaxed slightly.

"Can we start the engines yet?" Shaw asked.

I shook my head. "Not yet. Another twenty minutes, perhaps. Maybe longer."

"We must get to Hiroshima before it is light."

"I understand."

"With those yards destroyed they will have almost as much difficulty replenishing their ammunition as we have. It will make it more of an equal fight."

"I agree," I said. "And now, General Shaw, can you tell me what you hope to use to accomplish that destruction?"

"It is in the lower hold," he said. "You saw the scientists bringing it aboard."

"But what is it, this Project NFB?"

"I'm told it's a powerful bomb. I know very little more—it is *extremely* scientific—but it has been a dream of some scientists to make it since, I suppose, the beginnings of the century. It has cost us a lot of money and several years of research just to build one—the one in the lower hold."

"How do you know it will work?"

"I do not. But if it does work, it should, in a *single explosion*, devastate the best part of the airship yards. The scientists tell me that when it is detonated the explosion will be equal to several hundred tons of TNT."

"Good God!"

"I was equally incredulous, but they convinced me—particularly when three years ago they almost destroyed their entire laboratory with a very minor experiment along these lines. It is something to do with the atomic structure of matter, I believe. They had the theory for the bomb for a long time, but it took years to make the thing workable."

"Well, let's hope they're right," I smiled. "If we drop it and it turns out to have the explosive power of a firecracker we are going to look very foolish."

"Agreed."

"And if it is as powerful as you say, we had better keep high enough up—blasts rise as well as spread. We should be at least a thousand feet above ground-level when it goes off."

Shaw nodded absently.

Soon I was able to start the engines and the *Shantien's* bridge trembled slightly as we surged through the night at 150 mph with the wind behind us! The roar of her engines going full out was music to my ears. I began to cheer up and checked our position. We had not much time to spare. By my calculations we should reach the Hiroshima airship yards about half-an-hour before the first intimation of dawn.

For a while we were all lost in our own thoughts, standing on the bridge and listening to the rapid note of the engines.

It was Shaw who broke the silence.

"If I die now," he said suddenly, expressing a notion not far from the minds of any of us. "I think that I have sown the seeds for a successful revolution throughout the world. The scientists at Dawn City will perfect Project NFB even if *this* bomb is not successful. More of the *Fei-chi* will be built and distributed amongst other revolutionists. I will give power to the people. Power to decide their own fate. I have already shown them that the Great Powers are not invincible, that they can be overthrown. You see, Uncle Vladimir, it *is* hope and not despair which breeds successful revolution!"

"Perhaps," Ulianov admitted. "Yet hope alone is not sufficient."

"No—political power grows out of the erupting casing of a bomb like the bomb we are carrying. With such bombs at their disposal, the oppressed will be able to dictate any terms they choose to their oppressors."

"If the bomb works," Una Persson said. "I am not sure it can. Nuclear fission, eh? All very well—but how do you achieve it? I fear you may have been deceived, Mr Shaw."

"We'll see."

I remember the feeling of anticipation as the dark coast of Japan was sighted against the gleam of the moonlit ocean and once again we cut out the engines and began to drift on the wind.

I readied the controls which would release the safety bolts on the loading doors (the main bolts had to be drawn by hand) and let the bomb fall onto the unsuspecting airship yards. I saw ribbons of myriad coloured lights. The city of Hiroshima. Beyond it lay the yards themselves—miles of sheds, of mooring masts and repair docks, an installation almost entirely given over to military airships, particularly at this time. If we could destroy only a part of it, we should succeed in delaying the assault on Dawn City.

I remember staring at Una Persson and wondering if she were still thinking of her father's death. And what was Dutchke brooding about? He had begun by hating Shaw but now he was bound to admit that the Warlord of the Air was a genius and that he had achieved what many another revolutionist had hoped to achive. Ulianov, for instance. It seemed that the old man hardly realised that his dream was coming true. He had waited so long. I suppose I sympathise with Ulianov more than most now. He had waited all his life for revolution, for the rise of the proletariat, and he was never to see it actually taking place. Perhaps it never did. . . .

Shaw was leaning forward eagerly as we drifted high above the airship yards. He had one hand on the holster, a cigarette in his other hand. His yellow coolie hat was pushed back off his head and with his handsome Eurasian features he looked every bit a hero of popular romance.

The yards were ablaze with light as men worked on the battleships which were to be ready for the big invasion on Dawn City next day. I saw the black outlines of the hulls, saw the flare of acetylene torches.

"Are we there?" Once again the Warlord who had

changed history looked like an excited schoolboy. "Are those the yards, Captain Bastable?"

"That's them," I said.

"The poor men," said Ulianov shaking his white head. "They are only workers, like the others."

Dutchke jerked his thumb back towards the city. "Their children will thank us when they grow up."

I wondered. There would be many orphans and widows in Hiroshima tomorrow.

Una Persson looked nervously at me. It seems she had lost her doubts about the efficacy of the bomb. "Mr Bastable, as I understand it a bomb of this type can, in theory, produce incalculable destruction. Parts of the city might be harmed."

I smiled. "The city's nearly two miles away, Mrs Persson."

She nodded. "I suppose you're right." She stroked her neat, dark hair, looking down at the yards again.

"Take her down to a thousand feet, Height Cox," I said. "Easy as she goes."

We could see individual people now. Men moved across the concrete carrying tools, climbing the scaffolding around the huge ironclads.

"There's the main fitting yards." Shaw pointed. "Can we get the ship over there without power?"

"We'll be spotted soon. But I'll try. Five degrees, Steering Cox."

"Five degrees, sir," said the pale young man at the wheel. The ship creaked slightly as she turned.

"Be ready to take her up fast, Height Cox," I warned.

"Aye, aye, sir."

We were over the fitting yards. I picked up my speaking tube.

"Captain to lower hold. Are the main loading doors ready?"

"Ready, sir."

I pressed the lever which would release the safety bolts.

"Safety bolts gone, sir."

"Stand by to release cargo."

"Standing by, sir."

I was using a procedure normally used to lighten the ship in an emergency.

The huge ship sank down and down through the night. I heard a sighing breeze sliding about her nose. A melancholy breeze.

"Gunners make ready to fire. Return fire if fired upon." This was in case we were recognised and attacked. I was relying on the surprise of the big explosion to give us time to get away.

"All guns ready, sir."

Shaw winked at me and chuckled.

"Stand by all engines," I said. "Full ahead as soon as you hear the bang."

"Standing by, sir."

"Ready cargo doors."

"Ready, sir."

"Let her go."

"She's gone, sir."

"Elevation sixty degrees," I said. "Up to three thousand, Height Cox. We've made it."

The ship tilted and we gripped the handrails as the bridge sloped steeply.

Shaw and the others were peering down. I remember their faces so well. Dutchke pursing his lips and frowning. Una Persson apparently thinking of something else altogether. Ulianov smiling slightly to himself. Shaw turned to me. He grinned. "She's just about to hit. The bomb . . ."

I remember his face full of joy as the blinding white light flooded up behind him, framing the four of them in black silhouette. There was a strange noise, like a single, loud heartbeat. There was darkness and I knew I was blind. I burned with unbearable heat. I remember wondering at the intensity of the explosion. It must have destroyed the whole city, perhaps the island. The enormity of what had happened dawned on me.

"Oh my God," I remember thinking, "I wish the damned airship had never been invented."

## CHAPTER VIII

### The Lost Man

"AND THAT'S ABOUT it." Bastable's voice was harsh and cracked. He had been talking for the best part of three days.

I laid down my pencil and looked wearily back through the pages and pages of shorthand notes which recorded his fantastic story.

"You really believe you experienced all that!" I said. "But how do you explain getting back to our own time?"

"Well, I was picked up in the sea, apparently; I was unconscious, temporarily blinded and quite badly burned. The Japanese fishermen who found me thought I was a seaman who'd been caught in an engine-room accident. I was taken to Hiroshima and put into the Sailors' Hospital there. I was quite astonished to be told it *was* Hiroshima, I don't mind admitting, since I was convinced the place had been blown to smithereens. Of course, it was some time before I realised I was back in 1902."

"And what did you do then?" I helped myself to a drink and offered him one which he refused.

"Well, as soon as I came out of the hospital I went to the British Embassy, of course. They were decent. I claimed I had amnesia again. I gave my name, rank and serial number and said that the last thing I remembered was being pursued by Sharan Kang's priests in the Temple of the Future Buddha. They telegraphed my regiment and, naturally, they confirmed that the particulars I had given were correct. I had my passage and train fare paid to Lucknow, where my regiment was then stationed. Six months had passed since the affair at Teku Benga."

"And your commanding officer recognised you, of course."

Bastable gave another of his short, bitter laughs. "He said that I had died at Teku Benga, that I could not have lived. He said that although I resembled Bastable in some ways I was an impostor. I was older, for one thing, and my voice was different."

"You reminded him of things only you could remember?"

"Yes. He congratulated me on my homework and told me that if I tried anything like that again he would have me arrested."

"And you accepted that? What about your relatives? Didn't you try to get in touch with them."

Bastable looked at me seriously. "I was afraid to. You see this is not completely the world I remember. I'm sure it's my memory. Something caused by my passage to and fro in Time. But there are small details which seem wrong. . . ." He cast about with a wild eye, like one who suddenly realises he is lost in a place he presumed familiar. "Small details. . . ."

"The opium, perhaps?" I murmured.

"Maybe."

"And that's why you're afraid to go home. In case your relatives *don't* recognise you?"

"That's why. I think I will have that drink." He crossed the room and poured himself a large glass of rum. He had exhausted his supply of drugs while talking to me. "After being kicked out by my C.O.—I recognised *him*, by the way—I wandered up to Teku Benga. I got as far as the chasm and sure enough the whole place was in ruins. I had a horrifying feeling that if I *could* cross that chasm I'd find a corpse and it would be mine. So I didn't try. I had a few shillings and I bought some native clothes—begged my way across India, sometimes riding the trains, looking, at first, for some sort of confirmation of my own identity, somebody to tell me I really was alive. I talked to mystics I met and tried to get some sense out of them, but it was all no good. So I decided I'd try to forget my identity. I took to swallowing opium in any form I could get it. I went to China. To Shantung. I found the Valley of the Morning. I don't know what I expected it to be. It was as beautiful as ever. There was a little, poor village in it. The people were kind to me."

"Then you came here?"

"After a few other places, yes."

I didn't know what to make of the chap. I could not but believe every word of what he had said. The conviction in his voice was so strong.

"I think you'd better come back to London with me," I said. "See your relatives. They'll be bound to know you."

"Perhaps." He sighed. "But you know, I think I'm not *meant* to be here. That explosion—that awful explosion over Hiroshima—it—it spat me out of one time in which I didn't belong—into another. . . ."

"Oh, nonsense."

"No, it's true. This is 1903—or *a* 1903—but it—it isn't *my* 1903."

I thought I understood what he meant, but I could hardly believe that such a thing could be remotely true. I could accept that a man had gone forward in Time and been returned to his own period—but I couldn't believe that there might be an *alternative* 1903.

Bastable took another drink. "And pray to God that it wasn't *your* 1973," he said. "Science run wild—revolutions—bombs which can destroy whole cities!" He shuddered.

"But there were benefits," I said hesitantly. "And I'm not sure the natives you mention weren't, on the whole, well off."

He shrugged. "Different ages make the same people think in different terms. I did what I did. There's nothing else to be said. I probably shouldn't do it now.

Besides, there *is* more freedom in this world of ours, old man. Believe me—there is!"

"It's disappearing every day," I said. "And not everyone's free. I admit that privilege exists . . ."

He raised a silencing hand. "No discussions of that kind, for God's sake."

"All right."

"You might as well tear those notes up," he said. "Nobody will believe you. Why should they? Do you mind if I take a bit of a stroll—get some fresh air, while I think what to do?"

"Yes. Very well."

I watched him walk tiredly out of the room and heard his feet on the stairs. What a strange young man he was.

I glanced through my notes. Giant airships—monorailways—electric bicycles—wireless telephones—flying machines—all the marvels. They could not have been invented by the mind of one young man.

I lay down on my bed, still mulling the problem over, and I must have fallen asleep. I remember waking briefly once and wondering where Bastable was, then I slept till morning, assuming he was in the next room.

But when I got up Ram Dass told me that the bed had not been slept in. I went and enquired of Olmeijer if he knew where Bastable was, but the fat Dutchman had not seen him.

I asked everyone in the town if they had come across Bastable. Someone told me that they had seen a young man staggering down by the harbour late at night and assumed him drunk.

A ship had left that morning. Perhaps Bastable had got aboard. Perhaps he had thrown himself into the sea.

I heard no more of Bastable, though I advertised for news of him and spent more than a year making enquiries, but he had vanished. Perhaps he had actually been snatched through Time again—to the past or the future or even to the 1903 he thought he should belong in?

And that was that. I've had the whole manuscript

typed up, put it into order, cut out repetitions and some unnecessary comments Bastable made while he spoke. I've clarified where I could. But essentially this is Bastable's account as he told it to me.

*Note* (1907): Since I saw Bastable, of course, the air has been conquered by the Wright brothers and the powered balloon is being developed apace. Radiotelephony had become an actuality and I heard recently that there are several inventors experimenting with monorail systems. Is it all coming true? If so, for my own selfish reasons, I look forward to a world made increasingly peaceful and convenient, for I shall be dead before the world sees the revolutionary holocaust Bastable described. And yet there are a few things which do not coincide with his description. The heavier than air flying machine is an actuality already. People in France and America are flying them and there is even some talk of flying across the channel in one! But perhaps these aeroplanes will not last or are not capable of very great speeds or sustained flight.

I have tried to interest a number of publishers in Bastable's account, but all judge it too fantastical to be presented as fact and too gloomy to be presented as fiction. Writers like Mr Wells seem to have the corner in such books. Only this one is true. I'm sure it is true. I shall continue to try to get it published, for Bastable's sake.

*Note* (1909): Bleriot has flown the channel in an aeroplane! Again I tried to interest a publisher in Bastable's story and, like several others, he asked me to alter it—'put in more adventures—a love story—a few more marvels' is what he said. I cannot alter what Bastable told me and so I consign the manuscript to the drawer for perhaps another year.

*Note* (1910): Off to China soon. Might look for the

Valley of the Morning to see what it is like and perhaps hope to find Bastable there. He seemed to like the place and the villagers, he said, looked after him well. China *is* full of revolutionists these days, of course, but I expect I'll be safe enough. I may even be there when it becomes a republic! Certainly things are shaky and it's likely the Russians and Japanese will try to grab large chunks of the country.

If I do not return from China, I should be grateful if someone continued to try to get this published. *MCM*

## EDITOR'S NOTE

The above was the last note my grandfather made on the manuscript—or the last we have found, anyway. He did return from China, but doubtless he didn't find Bastable there or he would have mentioned it. I think he must have given up trying to get the book published after 1910.

My grandfather went to France in 1914 and was killed on the Somme in October, 1916.

Michael Moorcock, 1971.

# Award Winning
# Science Fiction Specials

| | | | |
|---|---|---|---|
| 00950 | **After Things Fell Apart** | Goulart | 75c |
| 02268 | **And Chaos Died** | Russ | 75c |
| 10480 | **Chronocules** | Compton | 75c |
| 47800 | **The Left Hand of Darkness** | LeGuin | 95c |
| 58050 | **Nine Hundred Grandmothers** | Lafferty | 95c |
| 62938 | **One Million Tomorrows** | Shaw | 75c |
| 65050 | **The Palace of Eternity** | Shaw | 75c |
| 65300 | **Past Master** | Lafferty | 60c |
| 65430 | **Pavane** | Roberts | 95c |
| 66100 | **The Phoenix and the Mirror** | Davidson | 75c |
| 67800 | **The Preserving Machine** | Dick | 95c |
| 76385 | **The Silent Multitude** | Compton | 75c |
| 79450 | **Synthajoy** | Compton | 60c |
| 88601 | **Why Call Them Back From Heaven?** | Simak | 75c |
| 89851 | **The Witches of Karres** | Schmitz | 75c |
| 90075 | **Wizard of Earthsea** | LeGuin | 75c |
| 94200 | **The Year of the Quiet Sun** | Tucker | 75c |

*Available wherever paperbacks are sold or use this coupon.*

**ace books,** (Dept. MM) Box 576, Times Square Station
New York, N.Y. 10036
Please send me titles checked above.

I enclose $.................... Add 10c handling fee per copy.

Name ......................................................

Address ...................................................

City..................... State.............. Zip........

Please allow 4 weeks for delivery.                          7

# ACE SCIENCE FICTION DOUBLES
## Two books back-to-back for just 75c

---

05595  Beyond Capella Rackham
**The Electric Sword-Swallowers** Bulmer

---

11182  **Clockwork's Pirate**
**Ghost Breaker** Goulart

---

11560  **The Communipaths** Elgin
**The Noblest Experiment in the Galaxy**
Trimble

---

13783  **The Dark Dimensions**
**Alternate Orbits** Chandler

---

13793  **Dark of the Woods**
**Soft Come the Dragons** Koontz

---

13805  **Dark Planet** Rackham
**The Herod Men** Kamin

---

51375  **The Mad Goblin**
**Lord of the Trees** Farmer

---

58880  **Alice's World**
**No Time for Heroes** Lundwall

---

71802  **Recoil** Nunes
**Lallia** Tubb

---

76096  **The Ships of Durostorum** Bulmer
**Alton's Unguessable** Sutton

---

78400  **The Star Virus** Bayley
**Mask of Chaos** Jakes

---

81610  **To Venus! To Venus!** Grinnell
**The Wagered World** Janifer and Treibich

---

# 10
## NOVELS BY
# ROBERT A. HEINLEIN

| | | |
|---|---|---|
| 05500 | Between Planets | 95c |
| 10600 | Citizen of the Galaxy | 95c |
| 31800 | Have Space Suit—Will Travel | 95c |
| 71140 | Red Planet | 95c |
| 73330 | Rocket Ship Galileo | 95c |
| 73440 | The Rolling Stones | 95c |
| 77730 | Space Cadet | 95c |
| 78000 | The Star Beast | 95c |
| 82660 | Tunnel in the Sky | 95c |
| 91501 | The Worlds of Robert A. Heinlein | 60c |

*Available wherever paperbacks are sold or use this coupon.*

- - - - - - - - - - - - - - - - - - - - - -

**ace books,** (Dept. MM) Box 576, Times Square Station
New York, N.Y. 10036

Please send me titles checked above.

I enclose $................Add 15¢ handling fee per copy.

Name ......................................................

Address ...................................................

City..................... State............. Zip.........

Please allow 4 weeks for delivery.